BOSS OF THE LONG T

Del Pearce was on his way to the town of
San Felipe for a break after six months
riding for a cow outfit, and he had no
intention of returning to Halley's ranch
until his wallet had resumed its customary
flatness. Fate, however, was riding on the
San Felipe stagecoach that day, not to
mention the pretty girl who captured
Pearce's eye and heart almost from their
first encounter, and two masked hold-up
men were determined that Pearce should
switch to a different destination at the end
of the line ... setting the scene for intrigue,
jealousy and murder.

BOSS OF THE LONG T

BOSS OF THE LONG T

by

Carl Mason

Dales Large Print Books
Long Preston, North Yorkshire,
BD23 4ND, England.

British Library Cataloguing in Publication Data.

Mason, Carl
    Boss of the Long T.

    A catalogue record of this book is
    available from the British Library

    ISBN   978-1-84262-505-7 pbk

First published in Great Britain in 1992 by Robert Hale Ltd.

Published in Large Print 2007 by arrangement with
Robert Hale Limited

Dales Large Print is an imprint of Library Magna Books Ltd.

Printed and bound in Great Britain by
T.J. (International) Ltd., Cornwall, PL28 8RW

One

Del Pearce shifted himself for the hundredth time on the lumpy seat of the Concord as it rattled over the rocky trail. The girl on the opposite seat was no less uncomfortable, but she gave no sign as she peered through the window at the wild landscape sweeping past. Once or twice, since she had joined the stagecoach at Dry Fork, Pearce had tried to catch her eye, but the girl plainly had been warned against strangers, or else she saw little to attract her in the lean, big-boned man in the dark range garb. At any rate, she had kept her eyes studiously averted after one swift glance at Pearce as she climbed into the coach. The third passenger snored in a corner, a fat, red-faced man, who had imparted to Pearce that he was on his way to San Felipe to introduce a new brand of cigar.

For mile after mile, the wheels of the coach scraped over hard rock and slithered through gritty sand and shale, while the morning sun lifted in a cloudless sky. Pearce slouched back in his seat and slanted the brim of his black sombrero across his face. He released breath in a heavy sigh and peered covertly at the girl from hooded eyes.

After a while she brought her attention away from the window and allowed her gaze to linger on Pearce. He, in turn, studied the tanned, oval-shaped features, admired the graceful curve of cheek and neck, lingered over his appraisal of her warm, full-lipped mouth. Beneath the dust-grey travelling suit she wore was a slim form, well moulded and extremely interesting to a man like him who had almost forgotten what it was like to hold a woman in his arms.

Six long months on a cow-ranch had fattened his wallet, and he was looking forward to this break from punching steers and planting fence posts. He would spend a few days in the big cow-town of San Felipe, and when the wallet had been reduced to its customary flatness, he would head back to the Triple X and sign on again. Big John Halley always kept a berth for him, prizing him as one of the best cowhands ever to straddle a Triple X pony.

This girl rocking along with him in the Concord made him all the more eager and anxious to reach the town as soon as possible. Even as he watched her, a slow stir lifted in his blood.

Their eyes met and he knew she had seen through his pretence of sleeping. A tide of colour stained her cheeks and she turned her face to the window again.

Pearce grinned, saying in a low voice: 'Mighty hard to sleep with this rolling and rocking going on.'

The girl vouchsafed no answer and Pearce shrugged, taking one of the drummer's samples from his pocket. He had just placed the cigar between his teeth, and was searching for his tin match-box, when hoofbeats cut in on the rattle and creak of the stage.

There was a stentorian shout, a gunshot, and then the brakes were grating the big wheels to a standstill in a cloud of yellow dust.

The girl stared at Pearce, her pretty face suddenly pale and frightened. The cigar drummer came awake with a start and almost rolled off the seat. 'Are we in San Felipe...'

Pearce was concentrating on what was taking place outside the coach. He heard someone order the driver to hold on for a minute while he had a look. Then a horse minced closer and Pearce saw a broad-shouldered man with scarf pulled up over the lower half of his face. He had a revolver in his hand, and it was aimed at Pearce.

'Hey, you... Yeah, you, friend. Come on out of there.'

Pearce swallowed hard. His right hand moved towards the gun at his hip, but the masked man made a warning motion that caused him to lift his arms into full view.

'You better heed me, mister. Come on out.'

Frowning, Pearce's glance touched the girl to see her lips tightly drawn. There was still fear in her eyes, but now there was wonder, too, and sympathy for him. He had little time to think about her as the coach door was hauled open and once again the road-agent repeated his command.

Pearce climbed out, saying as he did so: 'You're making a mistake. I'm a stranger to these parts.'

'We know you and that's enough,' came the crisp rejoinder. 'You any gear?'

Pearce stepped clear to see another masked rider holding his gun on the driver and shot-gun messenger. This one was saying: 'It ain't a hold-up, so keep your hair on, Dad.'

'My saddle's on top,' Pearce told the huskily-built one who watched his every movement as if he might make a try for his gun at any second.

'Get it down,' the messenger was ordered.

The saddle came down, and then Pearce saw the third horse, this one loose, a big chestnut with a starred forehead. His puzzlement grew.

'If you gents will just tell me what's going on...'

'Take off your gun-belt,' came the next brusque order. 'And do it real neat.'

There was nothing for it but to comply, and while Pearce stood glowering at the pair the other road-agent fired his revolver into the air and the stage team horses stretched into their harness, hauling the heavy vehicle into lumbering motion. Pearce watched it rock away in a pall of dust, feeling a tug in his breast as the brown-haired girl was carried beyond his reach. He turned to the masked men.

'Now let's hear what this is all about. And it better be good.'

The thin one slipped down and lifted Pearce's gun-gear. He buckled the belt about his own waist and nodded towards the chestnut.

'Throw your saddle up and get aboard.'

Pearce stood where he was, his grey eyes

smouldering. 'When I'm asked to do something I like to be asked the right way. Whatever your game is, I don't want any part of it.'

The two exchanged looks, and Pearce saw the broad-shouldered man's eyes smoulder dangerously above his scarf. He gestured with his revolver.

'We got orders, mister, and we got to carry them out.'

Pearce threw his saddle on to the chestnut and mounted. He cast one look away along the stage road to where the big Concord was dipping off a hummock. Then it was lost to view, and once again he thought about the girl inside. Those big blue eyes would haunt him for a long time.

The thin man rode out in front and his companion kept in Pearce's rear, close enough to draw and shoot if he tried to make a break for it. The stage had been moving into the west and this broken trail the men were following lifted into the north. So at least he knew the general direction he would have to take to reach San Felipe.

They reached a creek where the pair signalled their intention to water the stock. The thin one kept Pearce covered while the other took the horses in turn to the water to drink.

When the broad-shouldered man turned, his scarf was down and Pearce's eyes narrowed while he studied the blunt features.

'Now I'll know you again,' he commented.

'You've made a mistake.'

The man shrugged, grinning faintly. 'Name's Sam Moro,' he said. 'And that'll help better when you want to find me.'

Now the thin one tugged his scarf clear of his face. This rider was younger, with a pugnacious jawline and a generous sprouting of blond beard on his rather weak chin. His green-flecked eyes flashed a smile.

'Might happen we'll be better acquainted before long,' he told Pearce. 'Anyhow, I'm Jim Ferraza.'

Pearce tipped up the brim of his sombrero, still puzzled by their behaviour. 'As we appear to be in the mood for exchanging handles, you might as well know mine,' he drawled. 'Del Pearce.'

Jim Ferraza grinned and glanced at Sam Moro. 'What about that now?' he said. 'Climb up and let's get moving again.'

'I'm not moving another yard,' Del Pearce declared flatly.

'Don't make it harder, mister.' Moro's tone was cold, laced with impatience. He palmed his gun. 'We've got orders to deliver you, and that's exactly what we aim to do. Boss never said dead or alive, so I guess that won't matter much.'

For the first time, Pearce was touched by real fear. Jim Ferraza was smiling sardonically. He, too, was fondling the butt of his revolver. Pearce swallowed hard. 'I want a drink,' he said.

He went to the creek and knelt to scoop up a handful of water. Sam Moro moved over behind him, and Pearce sensed rather than noticed the man's nearness. Whatever game the pair were playing, he wanted no part of it. They must have mistaken him for someone else, and he just had to get away from them.

Moro's shadow fell on the earth beside him and part of the man was reflected in the creek as he bent to scoop another mouthful.

'You're mighty thirsty,' Moro complained. He yelped and tried to back off as Pearce's right hand reached out and snatched at his ankle.

Moro tried to kick Pearce in the face and Pearce lunged backwards into the creek, hauling Sam Moro on top of him. They hit the cold water and Moro's curses were cut short as Pearce swung a chopping blow that put the broad-shouldered man under.

Jim Ferraza was shouting from the bank, warning Pearce that he would shoot unless he held off. Sam Moro managed to clamber upright, water spilling from his clothing. He made a wild dive at Pearce and stumbled. Pearce caught him on the angle of the jaw with a crisp blow before he went under again. He was conscious of the flat crack of a six-shooter and a bullet splatted the water close to where he stood.

'Next one will get you square, mister,' Ferraza yelled.

Pearce stood until Sam Moro came out of the water. The stocky man's face was grey, and he belched sickly while the creek lapped coldly about his legs. He had lost his gun, and he groped around for it, finding it presently and ramming it into his holster. His eyes were baleful.

'Another trick like that and you're done, fella.'

Ferraza continued to hold his revolver menacingly while Pearce scrambled up the bank, followed by Moro.

Pearce suspected nothing until something heavy and solid took him in the base of the neck and sent him reeling to the grass. He lay for a while, writhing with pain and trying to hold his senses through the fog of confusion that threatened to blot out everything.

'You shouldn't have slugged him like that, Sam.'

'I'll split his skull, curse him,' the other spat. He nudged Pearce's ribs with his boot. 'Get up or I'll put your lights out, bub.'

Pearce groaned and tried to rise. He made it to his knees and rubbed his neck where Moro's gun barrel had hit him. A rough hand grasped his arm and hauled him upright. He found Moro scowling at him.

'Get on to your horse.'

Pearce staggered towards the chestnut. He would have to take it easy, watch every step. This Moro was as mean as a polecat and had a hot temper. Only for Ferraza he would have been at the wrong end of a real pistol-whipping. His boot found the stirrup, but it took another minute for him to summon enough strength to lift himself into the saddle.

'My hat...'

Ferraza handed it to him, sopping wet, and Pearce pulled it on, glad of the coolness against the base of his skull. He felt as if his neck might be broken. Ferraza mounted and told Moro to get out in front. The swinging motion of the chestnut helped clear Pearce's head. Moro was being really sick now and this gave him a vast satisfaction.

They moved into cattle country and the familiar sight and sound of cattle brought a prick of nostalgia to Pearce. He thought longingly of John Halley's Triple X. Moro dragged his horse to a halt. His clothes were steaming in the hot sunshine, and he bent a queer little smile on Pearce.

'No call to tell the boss about the fracas,' he suggested. 'Ain't that so, Jim?'

Ferraza shrugged indifferently. 'Quit worrying.'

'But we don't want him holding a grudge against us,' the stocky man persisted. 'After all, we might have to put up with him for a spell.'

'You wanted to crack his skull,' his companion reminded him. 'He ain't going to forget that.'

Pearce cut in on the exchange. 'I'll be real pleased if you gents tell me what's going on.'

'You'll find out soon enough,' Moro told him. He spat forcefully from the side of his mouth and gigged his horse into motion, falling silent, and once more Pearce tried to see to the bottom of the matter.

Presently they crossed a stretch of open range and Pearce saw a spreading hill. There was a ranch lay-out up yonder, a couple of large buildings and a scattering of smaller ones. Cattle grazed everywhere and he glimpsed two riders, a long way off, moving towards the rich green folds of the hills that lifted into the west.

'Looks like a sure enough cow outfit,' he said musingly.

'Sure it is,' Ferraza agreed with a sidelong look at him. 'What did you expect? You're in the Bighorn Basin country now, Pearce.'

'Never heard of it,' Pearce grunted. Why were they taking him to this ranch?

'You will *pronto*.'

Once again he asked himself what the whole business was about. What possible reason could these men have for taking him from the San Felipe stage and bringing him to this Bighorn Basin? He was pretty certain they were mistaken about his identity and had taken him for someone else. But to what end?

A short time later they were closing in on the sturdily-built ranch-house, and Moro and Ferraza took their horses to the porch where they dismounted, signalling for Pearce to follow suit.

A woman emerged from the open door-way. She placed one hand on the porch railing and with the other pushed a tendril

of hair back from her forehead. She subjected Pearce to a cool, probing scrutiny.

'Well, here he is, Miz Temple,' Sam Moro
proclaimed with a self-satisfied smirk. 'The
gent you wanted brought here. Pearce, meet
Lory Temple, boss of the Long T.'

Two

Lory Temple was dark, slim and vital. She was about twenty-five or so, Pearce calculated. The levis and blue checkered shirt she wore did little to hide the firm curve of thighs and the thrust of her high, full bosom. Pearce swallowed with difficulty, meeting the bold gaze that ran over him slowly, examining, appraising, judging. Her eyes held a glint of challenge as they lingered on his own.

'So you're Del Pearce?' She smiled and held out her hand. 'Pleased to meet you, Pearce.'

He took her fingers, conscious of a quick stir at the brief contact before she withdrew. She turned to Ferraza and Moro, smiled pleasantly. 'Thank you, boys. That will be all for now.'

'But he might try—'

'I can handle him, Sam,' Lory interrupted, firmness creeping into her tone. She waited until Moro and his companion moved off, taking the three horses, then put her attention on Pearce once more. 'Shall we go inside? I bet you could use a drink. Anyhow, it's cooler inside.' She appeared to notice his wet clothing for the first time. 'Oh, goodness! Did you fall into the river?' The question was posed innocently enough, and the dark eyes reflected the concern in her voice; still, Pearce detected faint amusement all the same.

'I took a ducking in the creek,' he told her. He decided to go carefully here. The woman knew who he was, so there was no ambiguity on that score. Somehow she had known he would be travelling on the San Felipe stage and had sent those two to hold it up and bring him here, by force if necessary. But why?

She directed him to the cook-shack, which was an appendage of the bunkhouse, and the Chinese cook took his wet duds, and draped pants and shirt close to the hot stove. Dressed again, Pearce returned to the front of the house as he had been directed. Lory Temple was waiting for him.

'Please come inside.'

He followed her along a hallway until she stopped outside a door. She looked at him then, smiling faintly.

'Promise me one thing before you go in,'

she said softly. 'You won't run away?'

'Not just yet,' he returned, angry at the odd huskiness in his voice.

'Thank you, Pearce.'

She was very close to him and he got a whiff of some scent from her hair. To Pearce, her smile was dazzling, infinitely provocative. She opened the door and led him into a room. Pearce came to an abrupt halt, seeing a blocky figure in a corner, sitting in the shadow.

'Pearce, this is my husband, Hugh.'

Pearce stood in the middle of the floor and stared at the man. Hugh Temple was broad-bodied. He held his massive shoulders hunched forward a little so that Pearce had an impression of tremendous physical strength. His face was grooved and lined, not an old face, but one that had known much suffering. The pale eyes reflected an alert mind and a vigorous personality.

Pearce searched his memory, wondering where he had seen this man before. He had a vague recollection of him astride a big horse, and he wondered at that, because Hugh Temple sat in a wheelchair with a rug thrown over his knees.

'Hello, Pearce.'

No hand was proffered and Pearce stood

as though rooted to the spot. A lot of thoughts and memories came back to him then, and he knew that somehow this big man had played a part in his turbulent past.

'I'm trying to place you, Temple.'

'Remember Attica, Pearce?' Temple's voice had a heavy, booming quality, full of energy and force. And then Pearce remembered him, remembered that day in Attica where Del Pearce was the town marshal and where a gang of crooks led by a cut-throat known as the Tucson Kid had tried to hold up a bank. The gang was really a bunch of cattle thieves, and they hadn't made a very good job of the bank hold-up. There had been a bloody gun battle and this big man Temple had been in the thick of it, with his six-shooter talking loud and clear for Del Pearce. Temple had wounded the Tucson Kid and Pearce had arrested him. The Kid had been put away in the hoosegow for four years.

He nodded. 'I remember you, Temple. I only saw you that one time. You left Attica before I could rightly say thanks.'

'I was in a hurry. There were cars in the siding with cattle aboard that I was bringing in on new grass. You left town yourself shortly after that, I heard.'

24

Pearce nodded again. Cowboy, gunman and lawman, his earlier years had been packed with danger and violence. At the age of twenty-seven he had finally sickened of the whole business and buried himself in the vast cattle country where John Halley ran his Triple X brand. He had thought no one would know him on the new range he had chosen, but somebody had remembered him, had seen and recognized him. And now this man Temple had had him forcibly removed from the San Felipe stage and brought here to settle a debt that was long outstanding. That was it, of course. He saw the whole thing clearly now. Hugh Temple had been crippled in some way, and he was in trouble. And he thought that Del Pearce would still be grateful enough to forgive that abduction and agree to help him out.

Pearce became aware of the woman at his side. This man Temple would be all of fifty, and yet the woman would be little more than half that age. He said to the big man: 'Why didn't you just send a message that you wanted to see me?'

'Don't blame Hugh, Pearce,' the woman cut in. 'He talked about you, told me the kind of man you were and how you had handled plenty of tough situations in your

25

time. He heard you were working on a ranch to the south-east, and then one of the boys said you had boarded the San Felipe stage yesterday morning in Beaverhead.'

'So you decided that I should be brought here to Long T?' Pearce finished tautly.

'I feared you would refuse if you were asked,' Lory said quickly. 'So I had a couple of my boys bring you here.'

'Lory has handled the outfit since – since this happened to me, Pearce,' Temple said by way of explanation. 'She told me she was going to send for you, but I warned her against it. I had a notion you wanted to leave your past life where it was.'

'Your notion was right, Temple. I was taking a trip to San Felipe to see the sights. I haven't been near a town for six months, and I thought I'd ride in on the stage for a shave and a hair-cut.' There was sarcasm in the smile he gave the woman. 'And I'd certainly have appreciated a proper invite up here instead of having a gun stuck in my face.'

'Pearce, I'm sorry,' the woman said. 'But I acted on the spur of the moment. I thought – I thought that if you were the sort of man Hugh said you were, you would understand when everything was explained to you.'

26

Temple pushed his wheelchair into the pool of light that came through the window of the room. 'I hurt my back,' he said. 'Got a bad toss off my horse. Doc says I might have to stay like this for a spell yet.' He grimaced his disgust. 'I told him to shoot me and have done with it. Maybe I'd have done it myself if it hadn't been for Lory here...' He mustered a smile and she moved to him and took his big hand in her own slender one. She stooped over him, kissed his cheek.

'Please don't talk like that, Hugh. I just want you to be able to walk soon, and ride as good as ever.'

Temple sighed. 'Well, sure as hell, if I don't–' He remembered the tall man watching him and grinned ruefully. 'Excuse me, Pearce. I was forgetting you were here. But when I think of what I used to be able to do, it kind of sticks in my gullet.'

'You did a heap that day in Attica,' Pearce assured him. 'It was the nerviest play I ever saw. And maybe you saved my life, into the bargain.'

'Aw, hell, mister, don't exaggerate. And that damned Kid vowed he'd get both of us!' He laughed. 'But, listen, Pearce, you're here by fair means or foul, and now that you are, I'm going to ask you a favour.'

'Hold on, Hugh,' Lory broke in. 'Who's boss of Long T anyhow?'

'Why, you are, of course, honey. For the time being, at least.'

'Good!' She gave him a warm smile. 'Well, now that we have – shall we say – persuaded Mr Pearce to come here, shouldn't I be allowed to settle the whole deal?'

'Lory, forgive me! You go right ahead in whatever way you fancy. You have a free hand until I can get around.'

'Thank you, Hugh,' she said sweetly. 'Mr Pearce, I promised you a drink which you haven't had yet. What do you feel like – strong stuff, or just coffee or tea for the present.'

'Better make it coffee,' Pearce grunted. He had been spinning the brim of his sombrero through his fingers, and now he drew his hat on as Lory turned to the door. The woman told him to follow her and he paused in the opening to look back at Temple. But the big man had drawn his chair up to the window where he could see across the front yard and over the green slopes that swept away from the ranch. He seemed to have forgotten Pearce already. Pearce's eyes crinkled in a frown. He closed the door behind him and went after Lory.

She hummed under her breath as she worked at the kitchen stove. Apparently she did the cooking for her husband and herself, while the Chinaman looked after the crew. She filled a pot from the pump in the stone basin and placed it on the heat. Pearce perched himself on the edge of a chair and searched for his tobacco. The waterproof pouch was intact but the papers were damp and useless, and when the woman noticed she went into another room and returned with a thick cigar.

'Thanks.' Pearce lit up and found the tobacco good. He studied the woman as she worked, watching her lithe, graceful movements with a growing hunger that was naked in his eyes when she turned suddenly to face him. She had been about to speak, but the words died on her lips, and for a moment she looked confused.

'I'll have the coffee in a minute.'

'I'm in no hurry at all, Lory,' he said quietly.

Her breath made a rasping sound in her throat. 'I'm Mrs Temple, Pearce. Or ma'am, if you prefer.'

'I'll call you what I like,' he said.

'You'll do precisely what I tell you, Pearce.'

29

'I'm not on your payroll yet,' he told her with a hard grin. 'So I happen to be my own boss just now.'

She moved closer to him, her eyes fiery, showing real spirit for the first time. 'You'll do what I tell you,' she repeated. 'You're here, and you'll not leave until I decide to let you go.'

Pearce threw his head back and laughed. 'Let me go? Well, I sure like that a whole bucketful! Now, you listen to me, Mrs Temple. I was on my way to town to have a blow-out. I've saved some money and I don't need to work for a spell. What do you want with me anyhow?'

'Hugh said you were a good man.'

'A good man for what – getting into trouble? Shooting a gent who steps out of line? Stealing a sick man's wife?'

'Stop it!' She was suddenly trembling, stiff-lipped, her right hand raised to strike him.

'Don't do it, Lory,' he advised. 'I'd hate to have to spank your pretty bottom.'

The blow was on its way when he reached out easily and trapped her hand. He held on, grinning wickedly into her face. 'Sorry,' he grunted. 'I couldn't hurt you even if I wanted to.'

'I'll tell Hugh you touched me.'

'Hugh's a cripple. He can't get out of that chair on his own.'

'He could shoot you,' she threatened, her breathing heavy, her breasts lifting and falling close to his chest.

'I don't give a damn about him,' he said throatily. 'But I sure hanker after his wife.'

He brought her to him and revelled in the softness and warmth of her, tasting the quick, eager hunger of her mouth. A long moment they clung, kissing fiercely. Pearce's hand slipped gently over the woman's shoulder, feeling the soft flesh under his fingers.

Someone rapped the door and Lory pulled herself free. She stared at Pearce for a second, catching the glint of amusement in his eye.

'Now will you let me go about my business?' he demanded softly. 'You can see that I'd be real bad for you, Lory.'

'I think I can handle you,' she said in a charged whisper. 'I know what you want, but I happen to want something, too.'

'Tell me about it.'

'Later.'

The door was rapped again and Lory drew it open. Jim Ferraza stood in the gap, a queer little smile warping his lips. He peered over the woman's shoulder at Pearce.

'Hugh said I'd find you here, Mrs Temple.'

'What do you want, Jim?'

'Leon Overacker and his foreman just rode in. They're out front.'

'Overacker!'

Pearce saw the way her anxiety registered. He wondered if this was some of the trouble he was expected to handle.

'What does he want, Jim?'

'Said he'd admire to see the boss,' Ferraza told her. 'Not you, Mrs Temple,' he added swiftly. 'Hugh. Overacker said he ain't going to parley with a woman. But Hugh told me to find you.'

Grimness and resolve replaced the earlier weakness. She said in a stiff voice: 'Would you care to overhear what Leon Overacker has to say, Pearce?'

Pearce's eyes clashed with Ferraza's. 'Should I?'

'If you're thinking of staying at Long T, yes, I think you should.' There was an underlying meaning there that was meant only for Pearce.

'No harm in listening,' he responded. 'But what about my coffee?'

'It will keep until you come in again.'

Lory gestured for Ferraza to precede her

and followed the cowhand.

Pearce sauntered into the hall and out over the porch, seeing a tall, horse-faced man astride a palomino. His companion was middle-aged, stocky, his weather-hardened features screwed up against the sunlight that was slanting across the hills. Pearce guessed the tall man was Leon Overacker. He was in his late fifties, in sober grey range garb. Pearce took note of the pistol hanging at his right flank. A rifle protruded from his saddle-sheath.

His foreman was a typical rider of the range country, in scarred chaps and hickory shirt. Pearce was conscious of the way their eyes drilled into him as he halted just a little to the left of the woman.

Jim Ferraza took up position on her other side, and Pearce was quick to see that Ferraza's right hand was resting on his gun butt.

'Mrs Temple,' Overacker began, 'I came here to see your husband.' He had a hard, dry voice that suited his stern mien and sober apparel.

'Hugh is unable to get around, as you well know, Mr Overacker. Anything you have to say must be said to me. I'm boss of Long T for the present.'

Overacker bowed slightly in acknowledgement. A steely glint entered his gaze. 'Very well then.' His tone became brusque. 'I've got to tell you that I won't stand for your men tampering with the river. You know they're building a dam in the hills at this very minute.'

'I'm aware of that,' Lory said firmly. 'In fact, it was I who gave the orders to build the dam.'

'But you can't do that, Mrs Temple!'

'The Bighorn rises on my land,' Lory reminded him. 'And I can do with it as I see fit. The dam's being built so that I can divert water through my own grass. My cattle in the north pasture have to travel too far to the river. I'm going to bring the water to them, which, as a cowman, you'll have to admit is good strategy.'

'But what about the herd I graze below the fork?' Overacker demanded, harshness edging his voice. 'My stock have always watered there.'

'I'm sorry, Mr Overacker, but I'm expanding, and I need water where I have grass.'

'Young woman,' the rancher thundered, 'I must tell you that I won't stand for it. It's against all the ethics of cattle country. I've ranged cattle in this basin long before you ever–'

'I know,' Lory interrupted him. 'Before I ever came to these parts at all. But I'm here, Mr Overacker, and my husband is ill. I'm carrying on for him.'

'Hugh Temple would never stand for a thing like this,' the other retorted. 'I want to see him right now.'

'I can see you from here, Leon.'

The voice came from the open window of Temple's room and they turned to look at the big man. His face was all that was visible, that and his great mop of shaggy hair.

'Hugh, can I come in and talk to you?'

'Sorry, Leon, I don't feel up to it. Anything that my wife says goes.'

'But, Hugh, do you know what this could mean? What has come over you, man?'

'Mr Overacker,' Lory said calmly. 'If you'll just listen to me, I have a proposition to put to you.'

Overacker swung on her, jaw thrust out aggressively. 'What sort of proposition?' he barked.

'I'm willing to take the herd you have grazing below the fork off your hands. At my price, of course.'

'The hell you say!' The rancher's eyes almost popped out of his head. He glared from the woman to her helpless husband at the window. 'Hugh, are you condoning all this?'

'She's the boss, I guess, Leon. I suggest you listen to whatever she has to propose.'

'I reckon they've got us treed, Boss,' Over-acker's foreman said grimly. His eyes sought out Pearce. 'You're new here, fella?'

Pearce dipped his head slowly, his gaze cool on the man.

'I wondered why Mrs Temple was getting so sure of herself,' the foreman drawled. 'Now I reckon I know.'

'What are you getting at, Grat?' Overacker snapped.

'The tall gent over there,' Grat said. 'That's Del Pearce, in case you don't know him.'

'Pearce, Pearce... Say, aren't you the fella that–'

'I used to do a lot of things,' Pearce inter-jected coldly. 'Right now I'm just standing here and listening to a lot of gabbing.'

'You aiming to do anything about it, Pearce?' the foreman snapped.

'Maybe, friend. Maybe not.'

'Pearce, you were never noted for getting mixed up in shady deals,' Leon Overacker flung at him. 'It happens that's just what you're getting into right now.'

'He might have another reason,' Grat said

in a derisive growl. His eyes shifted from Pearce to the woman at his side, and no one could mistake his meaning.

Pearce took a stride forward, but Lory grasped his arm, holding him. 'Take it easy, Del.' Then, to Overacker: 'That dam stays until I have the flow diverted. And my offer to buy your herd will be open until this time tomorrow.'

'Damn it, woman, have you no heart? You know we need that water. You know my beef will die of thirst. I've always had access to the Bighorn.'

'Sorry, Mr Overacker,' Lory said implacably. 'I'll be here this time tomorrow if you change your mind about selling.'

Overacker's patience ran out then and he stormed at her, shaking his fist. 'Do you realize what you're going to do?'

'I'm fully aware of what I'm doing.'

'Hell, you're not, woman. You'll start a range war, that's what! Hugh, do you hear me?'

But Hugh Temple had withdrawn from the window and Overacker exchanged looks with his foreman. 'Let's go, Grat. If this is how they want it, then they'll get what they deserve, and to blazes with fair play.'

Three

They watched Leon Overacker and his foreman until they had dropped to the flat beneath them and passed from sight beyond a fringe of willows. Jim Ferraza turned to Lory Temple, his eyes glittering in a way that made Pearce's fingers bunch.

'Well, Miz Lory, guess you told that old jackass where he belongs.'

'You can go now, Jim,' she said, a trifle stiffly. 'I've some things to discuss with Mr Pearce.'

Ferraza slanted a barbed look at the newcomer and moved away reluctantly. Pearce watched him go. He knew that if he stayed at this outfit for any length of time there would be trouble with Jim Ferraza. Lory walked back to the house and Pearce glanced over at Temple's window before following her. There was no sign of the big man.

In the kitchen again, Lory soon placed a meal on the table for Pearce, and he ate in silence under her steady regard. Presently, when he was almost finished, she said:

'What did you think of Leon Overacker?'

'He might prove to be a bigger enemy than you figure.'

'Then you'll stay here, go along with me?'

'Why did you bring me up here?' he wanted to know, lifting his head to look her squarely in the eyes.

'That has all been explained to you. We thought you'd be a good man to have around.'

'You mean that you're already preparing for war with Leon Overacker over water? So you could use an extra strong arm? But you'd better know that it's a long time since I've used my gun, shot at a man.'

'It's a long time since you kissed a woman,' she countered. 'The logic of your argument escapes me.'

He pushed his chair back and went to her, and this time the wife of Hugh Temple came easily into his arms. Her lips were warm and responsive as her arms encircled his neck. She said fiercely against his mouth: 'Stay and help me, Del.'

'Lory, I'm no wife-stealer, but I'd go to hell with you right now if you asked me.'

Again he sought her lips, but she pushed him from her gently, murmuring: 'Later. Del. It's too dangerous here.'

Over another cigar he listened to her talk about the ranch and was obliged to marvel at her spirit and ambition. Her father had always been poorly; ill health had dogged him for most of his life, and when his wife died he had simply faded away.

'Dad was a weak man really,' she said. 'But he did see to it that I had an education. But living with him and watching him struggle turned me against weak men for ever. I admire only strength, force, if you like. I admire a man who is tough and who goes after what he wants.'

'The reason you married Hugh?' he suggested.

'One of the reasons I married him. Hugh was a big man. He swept me off my feet and carried me here to the Bighorn Basin. I gloried in his energy and strength. He had grand ideas for making his Long T brand the finest ranch in the country. And then...'

'His accident, eh? He fell off his horse and hurt his back. And a man with a weak back isn't much use after all.'

He could see how his words were hurting her, but for some reason he wanted to hurt her, wanted to see her squirm. He recalled that big man in Attica who had swept aside everything before him and whose gun had put the Tucson Kid out of action. The man in the wheelchair in that other room was still big physically, except that his bigness was nothing but a pathetic husk.

Something of his thoughts must have shown in his eyes because Lory said: 'I do everything I can for him.'

'Yeah, I saw that. You look after him better than a mother would look after her baby. But is that enough?'

'It's all I can do for him,' she said simply. Her head dropped, and for a second Pearce saw her as Hugh Temple must have seen her on the day she stole his heart – slim, completely feminine, attractive as hell to a woman-hungry man, as most lonely cattlemen were on these vast, sparsely-populated ranges.

'What do you want of me?' he said.

'Stay here at Long T and work for me. I'm going to make this ranch grow as Hugh planned it would.'

'For Hugh, or for yourself.'

'A stupid question. I'm a strong woman and I need a strong man by my side to help me.'

First she had chosen Temple, and now she was choosing him. And he was sure that the man in the wheelchair caused her very little genuine concern.

'So far, I've managed to stay on the right side of the law,' he told her. 'I don't aim to break it.'

'Anything that I do will be inside the law,' she assured him. 'I know what my rights are, and I intend to stick by them.'

'This dam,' he said. 'Why build a dam at all?'

'The overflow finds its way into a natural watercourse that dried up years ago. It helps, but not nearly enough. I'm going to dynamite the rocks and change the course of the Bighorn completely.'

'That would be quite a job. You know that you could ruin everything, spill the water to hell and gone, and defeat your own ends?'

'I think I know what I'm doing. Would you like to ride out and have a look for yourself?'

'Yeah, maybe I should. But I haven't chipped in with you yet, remember.'

She came a little closer to him and there was gentle mockery in the depths of her lovely eyes. 'Look at me, Del,' she commanded.

'I've looked well enough,' he told her thickly. 'I can almost tell what you'll look like naked.'

'I make a hard bargain when I need to.

43

This must be done my way.'

'Well, I told you what I'd do for you. I'm crazy, I guess, but I can't help myself. Do you need to ask any more?'

'Good! And you've no pricks of conscience over – over what Hugh did for you one time?'

'I buried my conscience a long time ago, when it got too heavy to tote around. Anyway, I can't hurt Hugh now.'

'I'm glad you see it like that,' she whispered. 'All right, Del, then it's settled. Jim Ferraza has been acting foreman for some time, but you'll take over. You'll have to take over a lot, Del.'

'Let's go look at that river,' he suggested abruptly.

He went outside, and Lory soon followed him. She was dressed for riding and wore a flat-topped hat, boots, and jacket over a blouse. She looked almost boyish at this juncture. She brought Pearce to the corral and told him to take his pick of the stock. He whistled through his teeth, amazed at the magnificent horseflesh on display.

'You mean I can have my pick of the whole bunch?'

'Say, you sound like you've never seen so many ponies.'

'Ponies! Heck, that stallion must be all of sixteen hands.'

'Go in and catch him,' she ordered bluntly. 'But your surprise doesn't say much for your last boss' *remuda*.'

'John Halley keeps little else but working cow-ponies,' he told her, climbing through the fence with a looped rope and bridle.

She watched him from the top post, eyes flashing appreciatively as he went after the bay. A shadow fell at her side and she turned, frowning at Jim Ferraza.

'The stallion's my Sunday nag, Miz Lory,' Ferraza said. 'Is Pearce taking him out?'

'He likes the bay, Jim,' she told him, surprised at the irritation that rose in her. Ferraza fancied himself as something of a lady-killer, and several times Lory had caught him regarding her with a queer, speculative glint in his green-flecked eyes.

'But that doesn't say he has to take him.'

She stabbed a sharp glance at him, wondering at the slip of tongue. Ferraza had been getting bolder of late, but she had to admit that she had dallied with him once or twice, out of sheer boredom, discussing ranch matters, knowing that Ferraza enjoyed these long interviews.

'If Pearce wants the bay he can have him,'

she said. 'And I'd better tell you now, Jim, that I've just made him my foreman.'

'What!' Ferraza's jawline flattened and his narrow lips came together in a fine line. 'Are you sure you know what you're doing? Why, this Pearce gent has a rep for being a real bad actor. They say he ain't particular, neither, about how he handles women.'

Pearce came out with the bay just then. He said to Ferraza: 'Where did you put my saddle?'

'Better have a look for it,' was the cold rejoinder. 'Ain't nobody going to wait on you here, friend.'

'Jim!' Lory admonished.

There was mild amusement in Pearce's eyes as he came on to Ferraza and halted, holding the frisky stallion in with the rope. 'I could look if you tell me where you left it,' he said calmly. 'Better still, you could get it quicker if you went for it yourself.'

'Like hell I will!' the other retorted angrily. 'Lory, what kind of deal are you–'

Pearce had released the bay. At the same instant he brought his right fist swinging over in a short, crisp motion. There was a dull, splatting sound as knuckles connected with Ferraza's jaw and he reeled backwards.

'I'll tear you to pieces, mister,' he grated.

'You're a wind-blast, Jim,' Pearce taunted. 'Just get my saddle and we'll call it quits.'

Ferraza cursed furiously. He rushed his tormentor, a lean, agile man with plenty of power in his loose-limbed body. Pearce side-stepped, taking the brunt of Ferraza's blow on his elbow. Numbness ran along his arm. Ferraza swung around lightly. His next attack was a two-fisted onslaught that really put Pearce back on his heels.

The big bay snorted and minced off. Pearce steadied himself, taking a couple of hard slaps to the stomach before he managed to land a long, looping left hook to the point of Ferraza's chin. It was a good punch, and the cowboy blinked, momentarily dropping his guard. Pearce saw his chance then and stepped in, delivering two more wicked jabs to Ferraza's midriff.

The lean man retreated until he was up against the corral again, arms hanging, breath coming in harsh rasps. Pearce showed no mercy. He battered the cowhand until he could scarcely stand upright. Lory called on him to hold on, but he ignored her, delivering a final explosive punch that stretched Ferraza on his back.

'Go get my saddle,' Pearce wheezed.

'Del, please... Leave him alone. You've

47

hurt him enough.'

'He's got a lesson to learn, and he might as well get it over,' Pearce flung back. He put his boot to Ferraza's ribs, nudging him none too gently.

'Pearce...' Ferraza panted. 'I'll ... kill you ...'

'Get my saddle,' the big man was inexorable. Again he nudged Ferraza with his boot, and now the cowboy lifted himself up, grasping a corral post for support. He started towards the barn, walking unsteadily.

Pearce turned to find Lory studying him, something akin to revulsion in her eyes. 'Did you have to do that?'

'I reckon.'

'To prove how tough you are?' There was a trace of scorn in her voice. 'A strong man doesn't beat a weak one just to prove how big he is. I could have done without that exhibition, Del.'

'If you want me to ramrod this outfit, you'll have to like my methods,' he said flatly. 'Next time I speak to Jim he'll jump real quick.'

'Pearce, you're a fool after all. Jim will always hold this against you. You realize that?'

'He'll know I mean business.' He picked up his hat and rammed it on. 'I do things my way or I don't do them at all.'

Ferraza appeared with Pearce's saddle over his shoulder. The cowboy's face was streaked with blood and his right eye was red and swollen. He kept his eyes averted as he dropped the saddle to the ground.

Pearce said: 'Thanks, Jim,' and watched the man walk off wearily towards the bunkhouse.

Pearce saddled the bay and waited while Lory took out a pony. She rejected his offer of help and mounted, twisting away from the front of the ranch-house and angling into the west where the hills lifted in a series of brown and green ridges, beyond which towered rocky peaks.

Pearce went after her, thoughtful, a little grim smile playing at his lips. Perhaps his display of toughness had been too much for the woman and she would change her mind about hiring him. Which might not be a bad thing, he decided. The stealing of water was something that rubbed him the wrong way. And what Long T was doing was nothing short of stealing. Rivers and creeks should be allowed to flow freely and serve whatever cattle as could get to them. Pearce was certain that Lory was trying to force Leon Overacker to sell his stock at her price.

Lory Temple had visions of expanding and making Long T the richest spread in the country. Pearce had met other cattlemen with similar ideas, and their greed usually brought them to the brink of war with their neighbours before they came to their senses. Leon Overacker had struck Pearce as an honest cattleman, but a determined one as well, and he was sure that Overacker would fight to the last ditch for what he believed was right.

On a high, rocky shelf, Lory halted to let him catch up. Pearce stared away out and down to where the Long T buildings sprawled like so many dolls' houses. Cattle ranged as far as the eye could see, and once or twice he caught the dim shapes of riders.

'How many men do you hire, Lory?'

'About a dozen this time of year. We've got ten on the payroll at the minute.'

'And you couldn't find a suitable trouble-shooter among them?'

'I'm in no mood for making jokes,' she rebuked him sharply.

'I'm serious,' he told her. 'And I bet Ferraza could handle the crew as well as I could. I haven't even been tried. I might be a rank failure.'

'I doubt it.'

'So what you want right now is a fast gun on Long T to scare the pants off the likes of Leon Overacker. And remember,' he added with a malicious smile, 'I haven't killed a man in quite a while.'

She considered him for a moment, red lips pouting slightly. 'I hope you don't disappoint me, Del. I know that Hugh is banking a lot on you.'

'Maybe Hugh hit his head, too, when he fell. Did it ever occur to you that he might not give a curly damn any more?'

She frowned, then shrugged. 'You don't have to worry about that angle. You've only got to do what I tell you. We do have a deal? I intend to pay you a hundred a month, if that suits you.'

He whistled his amazement. 'What if I light out and leave you in the lurch afterwards?'

Colour suffused her cheeks and she looked away to where the green petered out in bare rocky slopes, ancient outcroppings of lava. 'I'll go after you and kill you, Pearce. I don't sell myself cheaply.'

She moved off and he followed her, slowing the bay when the ground became rough in the extreme. He dropped from his saddle when they entered a grey-walled pocket in

51

the cliffs. Pearce heard the noisy gush of water and soon saw a white race spill over a sharp ledge and plunge into a gigantic basin in clouds of spray. The water filled the basin, and the overflow formed a swift stream that eddied down the side of the mountain. He followed its path of descent through the grey slopes, and saw where the silvery ribbon wound, snake-like, through the lush grass of the lowlands. The woman gestured towards the south.

'Down there is Split Diamond graze.'

'Overacker country?'

She nodded. 'Don't worry too much about him. He has plenty of wells and water-holes.'

'But they dry up some in summer?'

'That's his problem. Long T and its welfare are mine.'

'This dam you've built...'

'We'll follow the river from here,' she told him. 'I want you to get the whole picture clear in your mind.'

They set off once more, descending now under the warm beat of the sun. Pearce got the feeling that they were being watched, but he could see nothing to justify the notion. He tried to shrug the worry off.

'Tell me something,' he said presently. 'You had a foreman before Jim Ferraza?'

She whirled abruptly, dark suspicion in her eyes. 'Why do you ask?'

'Oh, no reason. Just asking. But you had?'

She nodded curtly. She had no desire to discuss the subject.

'Did you fire him?' Pearce pressed.

'He had an argument with Hugh. I'd rather not talk about it.'

'So I see. Happens I'd like to hear about it, all the same.'

'What good will that do you?' she flashed angrily. 'Why can't you just mind your own business?'

'He fought with Hugh, didn't he? Because of you?'

She dragged her pony to a halt; her nostrils dilated. 'Luke Williams got too big for his boots... He tried to tell Hugh how things should be run at Long T.'

'And they fought over it, argued? Before Hugh had that accident? Before he was crippled?'

'Shortly afterwards,' she said gustily. 'Hugh and Luke had a row. Luke had a hot temper. They argued in Hugh's room and there was a shot.'

Pearce felt the short hairs rise on the back of his neck. 'They fought with guns?'

'Luke stormed in about something he

wasn't pleased with. He finished up by threatening Hugh. He pulled a gun...'

'And Hugh shot him?' Pearce urged tautly.

Lory let her head dip. He saw a tear appear at the corner of her eye.

'Did Luke Williams die?' Pearce demanded.

'Yes, he did. The sheriff came out from San Felipe. Hugh explained all that had happened, and the sheriff decided there was no need to take action. Luke had been overheard threatening Hugh. Hugh offered to go to jail, stand trial. But it transpired there was no need for that.'

Pearce blinked, trying to get rid of a mist that had suddenly clouded his eyes. Lory jabbed her heels into the pony's flanks and it went into a fast trot. Pearce nudged his own mount forward. They were entering a shallow draw when something snarled over his head a split second before he heard the wicked crack of a rifle.

Four

The bay stallion immediately went into a mad, plunging race and Pearce dragged hard on the reins as it dashed out in front of the pony. The rifle rattled again above the clatter of the bay's flying hooves, and he heard Lory scream in fright. They were soon partly shielded by the higher rocks, but they kept going until they reached the end of the draw.

Pearce leaped to the ground as Lory's pony raced up.

'No! Don't stop here,' the woman panted. 'Keep going.'

'Steady,' he snapped. 'There might be more than one of them.' He caught the pony's reins and dragged both mounts into a pocket where only a section of the draw and a patch of blue sky were visible. He helped Lory to the ground and she leaned against a rock while he brought his revolver clear and ventured to peer along the draw. 'I left my rifle with my saddle,' he fretted. 'Jim didn't take it out.'

'You should have collected your own gear.'

He signalled for her to be quiet while he listened. All was still, and after waiting for five minutes he started back the way they had come, on foot, disregarding Lory's appeal to stay where he was.

He soon reached a point where he could see the higher cliff ledges where the ambusher must have placed himself, but to gain their broken slopes he would have to cross a hundred feet of open ground. He had a hunch about the bushwhacker which he wished to put to the test.

He settled down again to wait, hoping the other would make a move into the open. There was no area visible where the man could have hidden his horse, so there must be clear ground somewhere at the back of the mass of rocks and boulders.

He was about to move on when he caught the dull glint of sunlight on steel, and he hunkered down once more, wondering if he had been spotted. Long minutes dragged by, and then something moved up yonder in a shadowed niche in the rocks. He flattened himself against the warm earth and raised his Colt so that he could use it at a second's notice.

He saw a man stand upright and peer out

across the sprawl of wasteland. The sun was in Pearce's eyes and he had no chance to recognize the marksman. A dislodged stone rattled down the face of the cliff and came to rest a few yards from where he lay. He held his breath then, seeing the figure freeze. Next, a rifle was being swung up, and a second later it blasted and a heavy bullet dug into the earth beside him.

Pearce waited no longer: he triggered a shot and saw the man scramble on over a higher out-thrust until he was silhouetted against the blue of the sky. Pearce fired again, but the man had dropped from sight on the other side of the grey ridge. He had no way of knowing whether he had made a hit. He guessed not. A scuffle behind him preceded the arrival of Lory. She was breathless as she sank down beside him.

'Del, are you all right?'

'I'm just fine,' he said wryly. 'I spotted the bushwhacker, but he's gone on over those cliffs.'

'Let him go,' she pleaded. 'It's likely one of Overacker's men.'

'You think they're gunning for me already?'

'They've never shot at my men before,' she declared worriedly.

'I was thinking it might be somebody else.'

'Who, Del?'

'Never mind,' he grunted. 'Let's get back to our horses.'

Pearce helped Lory aboard her pony and swung into his own saddle. They followed the course of the Bighorn down to another shelving of rocks. Here, a substantial dam had been constructed above what had been a dried-up stream bed. But now water flowed out of an ingeniously devised spout and gushed over granite outcroppings to enter the old water-course. To the right of the dam the proper outlet gaped darkly, only a thin trickle finding its way to the grasslands of Overacker's Split Diamond. No sooner had Lory and Pearce hauled up than two men appeared from a thicket, rifles at the ready.

'Howdy, Mrs Temple,' the foremost man called. He squinted curiously at Pearce. 'Anything wrong, Mrs Temple?'

'Someone was shooting back in the hills,' she replied. 'No need to worry, Burt. It might all have been a mistake.'

Burt nodded, his expression giving no indication of his thoughts. He and his colleague squatted on a hummock where they could keep their boss under surveillance while she was in the area. Pearce left them to have another look at the original course of the river. What water would reach Split Diamond stock would be next to useless. He could well understand why Overacker had ridden out in such a violent temper.

'Is this where you intend to dynamite?' he asked Lory when she joined him.

'Yes. Sam Moro is sure that when this bluff beneath us is shifted it will block the old course and turn the water across those pastures. The water-holes are full just now after the spring thaw and the rains we had recently. But later on they dry up and the cattle have to move too far to drink.'

'This looks a good thing for you, Lory, but it won't be so good for Overacker's Split Diamond.'

'He has plenty of range for his cattle,' she countered. 'I gave him the option of leasing me that grass bordering the river. It would have solved a lot of problems. But he simply laughed at me. Now I'm offering to buy the cattle and turn them on to my own grass. I can't be fairer.'

'Is this all you want me to see?' he asked at length.

'You've seen all that really matters for the time being. Sam will take you over the range later. He'll show you the entire lay-out.'

'I'll tell you something,' Pearce said while he spun a cigarette. 'If I was Leon Over-acker, you know what I'd do?'

'I can guess.' Her eyes hardened. 'But that's the difference between a man like you and a man like Leon. He'll talk and talk, perhaps shake his fist a little. But that's as far as it will go.'

'He's bound to have his limits of patience,' Pearce suggested soberly. 'If he does decide to go to war, it'll be an all-out affair, with nothing barred. Don't forget, he could hire gunhands, too.'

'Do you think that I hire gunmen?'

'They're certainly no angels. Neither am I. But Overacker could play the same game.'

'Just let him,' she said with determination. 'I know what I'm doing. I know where I'm going, and no one is going to hold me back.'

'If one of those rifle bullets had reached you, it would have held you up a mite,' he counselled. 'Only, I figure the lead was meant for me. Somebody doesn't want me around Long T.'

'You're thinking of Jim?'

'I'm thinking of him,' he admitted grimly. 'He's the sort that either stays tramped under when you step on him or else decides to stab you in the back. One thing's for sure

– he'll never meet me in a square do.'

They left the dam where the water boiled and seethed and roared, and soon reached the upper reaches of the Long T holdings. Far below them they could see the spread of the ranch buildings and now Pearce recalled what he had learnt from the woman about the death of her previous foreman.

Luke Williams had died at Hugh Temple's hand, and it seemed that no one could prove Temple had shot Williams because he had been playing around with his wife. He glanced at the woman, trying to see her in a different light. It was entirely possible that she might entice a man to her bed and then stand by while her husband shot the unfortunate victim. Lory could lay a trap for most men; she could watch the jaws snap shut with that secret smile at her lips.

She turned and caught his gaze, smiling so that she duplicated the picture in his mind. How long would it be before Hugh Temple would feel justified in calling Del Pearce to his office and blasting him with a shotgun?

'You're not worried too much about that ambush?' she queried.

'Not overly.'

Her voice dropped. 'I don't want anything to happen to you, Del.'

'That's nice to know. I don't neither. I admit I've still half a mind to catch the next stage travelling to San Felipe.'

'You'd break your word to me? But, you promised...'

'I guess I'll go along with you, Lory,' he said. He added wickedly: 'At least until I tire of you.'

She kicked her pony forward at that, fire leaping into her cheeks, and Pearce laughed outright, pushing the bay on down to the front of the ranch buildings. He was in time to see Jim Ferraza turn a grey horse into the corral.

Ferraza tried to hurry off to the bunkhouse, but Pearce put the bay in behind him and the cowhand twisted aside. He carried a Winchester rifle, and when he turned to Pearce he looked frightened.

'Hold on, bucko,' Pearce said breezily and slid from the stallion. 'I want to ask you something.'

Ferraza forced himself to look into Pearce's slate-grey eyes. He said tautly: 'What's on your mind?'

'Where have you been, Jim?'

'I'll answer to Lory, but not to you,' Ferraza retorted.

'You'll answer to me, fella, and you'll do it

pronto. And as from now, you'll stop calling Mrs Temple "Lory".'

Dark colour suffused the other's features. His eyes glinted. 'Don't press your luck too far, friend. What are you driving at?'

'Somebody took a shot at me up in the hills,' Pearce told him. 'Above the dam.'

'I heard a couple of rifle shots,' Ferraza said. Anger was crowding out his initial fear. 'But I was nowhere near.'

'I just hope you weren't, Jim, for your sake. I treat bushwhackers the way I treat diamond-backs.'

'I've got no fight with you, Pearce. I don't hold a grudge, if that's what you're thinking. And if I wanted to make a try for you, I'd do it where you could see me.'

'I'd sure like to believe you.'

'Whatever you please.' Ferraza spun on his heel, making for the bunkhouse.

Pearce off-saddled the bay and turned it into the corral. Lory brought her pony over and he knew she had heard the exchange.

'You think it might have been Jim, don't you?'

'I've a hunch it was nobody else,' he admitted.

She gnawed her underlip briefly. 'I'll fire him. I can't risk having you shot in the back.

Anyhow, I never really trusted Jim.'

'Don't fire him on my account, Lory. You might need all the men you can get before long. Building that dam will make you the least popular female on this range.'

'Does that go for you as well?'

His smile was crooked. 'When it does, you won't see my tracks for dust.' He prepared to leave her.

'Where are you going?'

'I'm going to have a little talk with your husband.'

'Goodness, no... Don't do that, Del. Hugh mustn't be worried about the ranch affairs.'

'I'm not going to worry him,' he said, raising a mollifying hand. 'At least I hope I won't. See you later.'

He strode off towards the house, spurs clinking. Lory watched his wide shoulders, biting her lip once more in real vexation. She started after him, intending to plead with him to stay away from Hugh, but Pearce was already ducking through the doorway of the house.

He halted outside Temple's room and paused, listening in case someone was in there with the big man. Then he rapped with his knuckles and Temple's deep voice boomed almost at once.

'That you, honey?'

Pearce twisted the handle and opened the door. Hugh Temple was in his chair. It was easy to see that he had been at the window. Pearce could scarcely conceal a start when he noticed the army telescope in the man's lap. How far could he see up the basin with that glass?

'Ah, it's you, Pearce... What brings you here?' He sounded surprised.

'I want to ask you a couple of questions if I may, Hugh,' Pearce began cautiously.

'I see! Lory runs things, you know. If you intend to work for us you'll have to take her orders. I'd better tell you that I never interfere.'

'I gathered as much. I'm not disputing that. But I must ask if you've thought about the trouble this dam could bring on your head.'

'I see!' the big man repeated. His smile held no amusement. 'I gather that you don't exactly think it's a good thing?'

'Hugh, you're a cowman first and foremost. Leon Overacker's a cowman and a pretty square one, I'd say. You understand how his stock will suffer if the scheme goes ahead?'

'So you didn't believe I was capable of

something so petty? But it isn't petty. It's very important to Long T. That rock's going to be blown out, and there's nothing more to be said on the subject.'

'You know what it'll mean for Overacker's stock? I guess you also know you could start a range war over that river.'

Temple laughed. It was a hard, booming sound that ran over the room. 'You're looking on the dark side. It's your lawman's training, I suppose, weighing up the different angles. Listen, why not just do as Lory asks you, instructs you? Has she discussed wages?'

'There's no argument there. The pay's more than generous.'

'You just bet it is, mister! You've never earned money like that on a cattle outfit.'

'I was thinking of other things besides money, Hugh. What about the value of a man's life?'

Temple sobered and his jawline hardened. A bleakness entered his eyes, and suddenly Pearce felt he was staring at a blank rock wall.

'I'd never hold a man who didn't want to stay,' he said tonelessly. 'You can even forget what happened in Attica.'

'I don't forget favours easily. You should

know that by now.'

'Maybe I know you better than you know yourself. Eh? What about that? Stay then. Stay for as long as you like. If you take the notion to leave, just tell me you're going. I figure that's a fair offer.'

'It's almost too good, and you know it, Hugh. It gets me to thinking about this and that. Especially about why you had to shoot the last foreman you had here.'

He might as well have struck the big man across the face. Temple reeled back in his chair, staring, mouth hanging open. He appeared to be looking at some particularly ugly memory that persisted in haunting him. It was a moment before the shock and distaste subsided and a forced smile broke the stern lines of the mouth.

'That was unfortunate, Del. Williams was a hasty-tempered character. We argued and he lost his head. He was foolish enough to try and draw on me. Had he known me of old he'd never have tried such a trick. I've regretted that day ever since.'

'I'm sorry to open an old sore. Could I ask you something else, Hugh? How long have you been in that chair?' Pearce framed the query in a low, measured voice.

A deep sigh ran around the place, causing

a chill to touch Pearce's spine. Temple spoke with bitterness. 'Almost a year now. Do I have to tell you what it has been like, especially married to a woman like Lory?'

Pearce wished he had kept his mouth shut. He nodded. 'I'm real sorry, Hugh.'

The big man waved an arm in a fierce gesture. 'I don't want your sympathy. I don't need anybody's sympathy.' He spun his chair away back to the window. Then: 'I saw you fight with Jim. You'd sure as hell better watch him, mister. He's more dangerous than a rattlesnake.'

Pearce started to respond to that, paused, and changed his mind. He said instead: 'Thanks for the tip.'

He was drawing the room door shut behind when he raised his head and saw Lory in the hallway. She was close enough to the room to have overheard what had been said. Her eyes glowed like coals.

'You thought he'd give you a different reason for shooting Luke Williams, didn't you? Did your dirty mind suggest there was something between Luke and me?'

He refused to answer that. 'I like to know if the ground under me is firm or if I'm walking on quicksand,' he said cryptically. 'Also, I wanted to find out something else about Hugh.'

'Such as what?' Her tone was scathing.

'Never mind,' he said. 'I'm not sure that I got the answer I needed.'

'If you're through with my husband I'll show you to your quarters,' she said briskly and preceded him along the hallway to the front door.

'I saw Ferraza heading for the bunkhouse,' he told her. 'I suppose I can bed down on any vacant bunk?'

'There's a cabin,' she jolted him by declaring. 'Luke Williams preferred to use it, and maybe you will, too.'

Thoroughly intrigued, he went across the yard and skirted the barn, forge and other outbuildings. They met no one on the way, and finally Lory pointed to a small log affair squatting beneath a lonesome cottonwood tree.

'There's your quarters, Del. Let me show you.'

He allowed her to lead him on to the cabin, and when he reached it he turned to look back at the main buildings. The cabin would be invisible from every angle over there except from one small window at the end of the house. Lory followed his gaze, appeared to read his thoughts.

'That's my bedroom,' she said, and added after a pause: 'And Hugh's. But most nights he sleeps in that other room by the open window. He doesn't sleep much and likes to watch the range by moonlight.'

Pearce turned to the cabin making no comment. A horseshoe on the end of a length of chain, then dropped into a large hook, sufficed for a lock.

'There's a wooden bar on the inside,' the woman told him and pushed the door open.

Inside the furnishings were sparse and functional: a chair and a bunk built into the wall, a small stove, table, cupboards. A shelf with an empty whisky bottle.

'Do you like it?'

'Suits me fine, I guess.'

She stood before him, just inside the doorway, that queer little provocative smile back on her full, red lips, and once again Pearce's blood hammered through his veins.

'Hugh has a glass,' he said. 'And a gun.'

'He can't get out of that chair without my help. Are you frightened of him, Del?'

'I don't scare easy.' His voice sounded thick in his throat. His desire for this woman was almost overpowering; it wiped out all other considerations.

'I'll see you tonight,' she said and slipped

away, leaving him staring after her, wondering what fate had decided he should board that stage for San Felipe.

Another vision came up before him then: that of a sweet-faced girl in a dust-grey travelling outfit who showed real concern for him when Sam Moro and Jim Ferraza had taken him off the stage.

He tried to kill the memory of her with thoughts of the desirable wife of Hugh Temple, and was surprised when he failed.

Five

There was still plenty of light in the sky when he took the bay stallion out of the corral and saddled up. He threw a look at the front of the house as he settled in the saddle, but there was no one about, no sign of Hugh Temple at the window of his room. But he was pretty certain that Temple would spot him before he had gone far.

With the big man in mind, he swung away from the front yard and angled around the long, low-roofed bunkhouse, leaving the lay-out at a point where there would be small chance of anyone following his movements.

He had no real reason for riding off beyond feeling some need to get away on his own for a while, so that he might gain a fresh perspective. Yet, when he came to a bend in the wagon trace he followed a long time later and saw the muddy river-bed, he halted and smoked a cigarette while he pondered on Lory Temple's scheme.

The bed of the watercourse was still damp, attesting to having been deprived of water only recently. On the opposite bank, he saw Split Diamond cattle shuffling through the grass to a well-trampled drinking spot. He smoked while a bunch of animals came down the bank and entered the river-bed, seeking for water. He frowned at their obvious puzzlement and disappointment, and one big curly-horned steer lifted its head and lowed plaintively.

A cowman first and foremost, it pained Del Pearce to watch the plight of the cattle, and he wondered how Leon Overacker could be so patient. Soon these beeves would wander away in their search for water, and the Split Diamond men would have a tough job keeping them on home graze.

He went along the bed of the Bighorn, not thinking of the miles he had covered, until he came to another wagon road with a signboard pointing into the south-west. *'San Felipe – 20 miles'* it read, and he wondered if he could make it to the town and back before darkness. The thought occurred to him that he had no business in San Felipe now that he would be staying at Long T. But once again he was plagued by the vision of that girl on the stage. She might still be wondering what had happened to him. Of course, the hold-up would have been reported to the local sheriff, and the law might be hunting for the road-agents at this very minute. It was most certainly his duty to see the sheriff and make it known that he was safe and sound, if slightly contaminated by the air in these parts.

He gigged the bay over the wagon road, deciding to have a look at the town anyhow, and if he happened to run into the girl... Well, that angle could take care of itself.

The road cut along under some beetling cliffs that lifted on his left, and after a while he fancied that hoofbeats were beating, more or less, in time with those of the bay. Thinking that it might merely be a play of echoes, he paid no more heed until he reached a point where the bluffs sheered off and the road dipped over a flat stretch of rangeland. Here, he looked back and upwards, and was in time to spot a lone rider beyond the reddening skyline.

He reined in, wondering if someone had followed him the entire way from Long T headquarters. When he thought of Jim Ferraza his mouth hardened. If Ferraza was determined to trail him wherever he went he would soon disabuse him of that notion. He watched the dark outlines of the bluffs, hoping to spy the rider again as he moved to lower ground. Nothing more showed, and this strengthened his conviction that he was being followed.

He nudged the bay on, from time to time looking backwards. There was no cover to screen a horseman now, and he could easily see anyone on his back-trail, at least while the daylight lasted.

His preoccupation precluded all else until a buckboard suddenly rocked round a bend in the road coming towards him and he slowed, recognizing the tall man on the driving seat and his companion. Leon Overacker would have sent the buckboard thundering on past him, leaving little room for anyone else, had not Pearce hauled out in front of the team, so that the two horses were obliged to prance to a halt.

The Split Diamond owner mouthed a surprised oath and glared angrily at him, eyes smouldering. But it was the rancher's travelling companion at whom Pearce gaped with wildly-beating heart.

'You!' he croaked. 'Why, I never dreamed...'

'Willa, do you know this man?' Overacker barked.

The girl in the dust-grey outfit at Overacker's side appeared equally stunned at the meeting. For a long moment she was incapable of answering the rancher. Then a glad smile brightened her face, causing Pearce's heart to stop for an instant.

'Oh, you're safe after all!' she cried. 'I'm so glad. Did those men harm you?'

'No, no, they didn't,' he assured her quickly, adding to Overacker's amazement: 'I hope you had a good journey to San Felipe.'

'Thank you, I had. Only–' She broke off to glance at the tall man on the seat beside her. 'Uncle was a little late coming for me, and I thought at first he had forgotten to meet me.'

Leon Overacker finally found his voice. 'Willa, do you know this – this man?' he grated while his eyes burned on Pearce.

'But he's the man I told you about, Uncle Leon. The one who was on the coach when the bandits held us up and forced him to go with them. I was sure they were going to – to kill you,' she added, serving only to cause her uncle greater puzzlement.

'Pearce, could I ask you what's going on here?' the rancher demanded harshly. 'If you've been trying some game on with Willa...'

'Overacker, I just met Miss – Miss–'

'Overacker,' the cattleman spat grudgingly. 'She's my late brother's daughter and

77

she's just come back from a visit east. I–'
But here the rancher's teeth came together
and his eyes burned dangerously. 'I don't
think it's any of your damn business, Pearce.
Willa, we'd better be getting on home...'

'But, Uncle, do you know this gentleman?'
The girl was pale by then. The eyes that
regarded Pearce from under the brim of her
bonnet were clouded with doubt and worry.

'I know him all right,' the other growled.
'But I'm not going to explain just now, not
until we reach home.'

Overacker raised the ribbons, preparatory
to urging the matched greys into motion.
He said to Pearce in a low-pitched voice:
'Stay away from my niece, mister. It's the
first and only warning you'll get.'

Pearce touched his hat to the girl, murmuring:

'Pleased to have met you again, Miss
Overacker, and I hope–'

'You can hope nothing, damn you!' Overacker snarled and sent the team lurching
forward, slapping the ribbons over the backs
of the greys. 'Just stay away from Willa or
you'll be sorry you were born.'

The buckboard rocked on past and Pearce
was forced to drag the bay to the edge of the
road. When the vehicle and its passengers

were nothing more than a cloud of crimson-tinted dust, he pushed his battered sombrero to the crown of his head sighing, and wondering at the cruel whims of fate.

'It would just be my luck,' he fretted. 'And she looks even lovelier, now that I've seen her out in the open...'

He glanced along the trail that wound on to the town, trying to reach a decision. He had not asked Willa Overacker if she had reported the stage hold-up to the sheriff, and Overacker hadn't given her much time to tell him. But he felt that it didn't matter much now. He had met the girl sooner than he'd expected, and learned who she was.

Turning about on the road, Pearce headed back towards the fork where he could angle out for the Long T. When he came to the bluffs he saw where Overacker had turned off for his own ranch. He sat for a while, watching the buckboard pass over a hill and once again dip from view. Then he gave his attention to the bluffs, hoping for a sighting of the man who had been trailing him. He searched around at the base of the cliffs, thinking he might find tracks that he could follow, but it seemed as though his tracker had been content to venture this far before turning back the way he had come. He tugged his hat down his head and nudged the bay into the direction of Long T. There was no real need to head for town just now.

He journeyed back to the ranch head-quarters in leisurely fashion, while he reviewed events since he had been abducted from the San Felipe stagecoach. He had allowed his desire for a woman to warp his reason to the extent of agreeing to hire on for an outfit that was set on making trouble for neighbouring ranchers. Nothing good would come of it: of that he felt sure, and he had an urge to ride out now while the going was good, before he committed himself irretrievably. But the horse he rode was not his own, and anyhow, he could hardly pull out without giving Lory Temple ample reason for doing so.

It was dusk when he rode into the yard of Long T and turned the bay loose once more. He was moving away from the corral when Lory appeared from the house. She called his name and he waited until she drew level.

'I was looking for you, Del...'

'I took a ride,' he answered briefly.

'Not to San Felipe?' He detected a catch in her voice and smiled faintly in the gloom.

'No. Just along the road a piece. Say, did

you send somebody after me when I left?'

'Of course not! Why should I do such a thing? I didn't even know you had gone. Did someone follow you?'

'I don't know. I'm not sure. Maybe it was just a notion.'

'I came out to find you for supper.' Her tone changed subtly the way it could, became intimate. 'Then I'd like you to meet the boys.'

'Must I do that just now?' A weariness lay on him at this juncture. He needed time to rest, more time to think and formulate plans.

'Of course you must. Get it over with as soon as possible. But not just yet.'

She took his hand in her own, pulling him towards the house. Her fingers were strong, cool, reassuring. They exerted some animal magnetism that plucked at the core of his being. He glanced towards the window of Hugh Temple's room, but it was in darkness. The gloom was too thick for Temple to see anything even if he did happen to be spying.

Lory released his hand when they reached the long gallery, and Pearce froze when a figure stepped out of the shadows. Instinct made his fingers fall to the gun at his hip. He pulled a hard breath to his lungs on recognizing Jim Ferraza.

'Take it easy,' Ferraza said.

'I'm doing exactly that,' Pearce responded in a slow drawl.

'Jim, what on earth...What is it now?' Lory demanded peevishly.

'I tried to find you, Miz Temple. I just got back.'

'Is everything all right?'

'Burt says he spotted a couple of horsemen scouting in the high rocks,' Ferraza disclosed in a rush. 'He figured they might have been getting set to wreck the dam.'

Lory's laugh was a small, explosive burst of scorn. 'Burt's imagining things, Jim. Overacker has too much sense to try anything like that.'

'You don't want me to take a couple of the boys up there?' Ferraza suggested.

'That isn't necessary. Listen, Jim, I'll be bringing Pearce over to the bunkhouse later to introduce him to the boys. Tell them to hang around.'

Ferraza nodded, staring at Pearce. 'I guess they'll be real pleased to meet him.' He dipped his head and melted away into the darkness.

Pearce was watching the spot where he had vanished when Lory touched his arm. If the rider up in the rocks hadn't been

Ferraza, he thought, then it must have been one of the Split Diamond men who had been watching him.

'Del, your supper won't keep hot.'

'Don't you think that Leon Overacker might just be angry enough to make a try at the dam?'

'Are you getting scared?' she demanded softly.

'It would be no laughing matter. I still think you're inclined to underestimate that gent.'

'Time will tell,' she said lightly and went through the doorway, Pearce following her after another probing look over the dark yard.

Much later, he lay on his bunk in the cabin and stared at the dark roof. There was a lamp on the table but he hadn't bothered to light it. Outside, the night was still and the heat of the day lingered in the air like a sultry memory. He thought of the men he had just left in the bunkhouse, reflecting on the cool, aloof reception they had given him. They were a hard bunch, without doubt, and Sam Moro appeared to have as much sway with them as Lory had herself. Moro was a cagey character and he had shown little enthusiasm when Lory announced her range boss. Moro would be a man to watch also. There was every chance that he resented his presence here at Long T as much as Jim Ferraza did. Moro had illustrated his brash temper when he had got that ducking in the creek, and Pearce felt he would be as likely to try for a shot in the back as Ferraza.

He lay for a long time, smoking, allowing his thoughts to shift as they would, still trying to make up his mind about this queer set-up, the odd deal he was expected to honour. That dam was a hellish thing, a symbol of all that was worst in cattle country, and he was sure that Lory was making what could prove to be the biggest mistake of her life.

He tensed when a sound reached his ears. Silence rushed in afterwards, but then he heard it again, the soft padding of feet. He knew when someone was at the door and lifted his Colt, thumbing the hammer back gently.

'Del...'

He breathed deeply, letting the gun slide back into its sheath. He had taken the precaution of barring the door in case he fell asleep, and now he lifted the thick wood from its sockets and drew the door open.

Lory wore a shawl over her shoulders and glanced carefully around her before stepping into the cabin. Pearce felt a quiver run through him as he replaced the bar in its sockets.

The mixture of starlight and moonglow filtered through the small window and struck her face as she laid the shawl aside. Her face was pale, beautiful, almost ethereal in the soft radiance. Her eyes glowed.

'Well,' she said with a little nervous laugh, 'here I am.'

'You're running a big risk. Are you sure that Hugh–'

'I've just left him. He's in his room, smoking and reading. He reads a lot, sometimes well into the morning.' She laughed again and now there was mockery in the sound. She was fooling Temple and she was getting a big kick out of it.

Pearce recalled once more what he had heard about Luke Williams. This had been Williams' cabin. Here he had slept alone and here he had ample opportunity to meet Lory just as he, Del Pearce, cowman, lawman and gunslinger, was meeting her now.

'What's the matter, Del?'

'Nothing much. I was just thinking.'

'You're worrying about Jim again? Well,

you don't have to. I sent him up to Burt and Joe with supplies. He'll be gone for a few hours.'

'I'm not thinking of Ferraza,' he told her.

'What is it then? Are you worried about Hugh, or...' She broke off, her laughter washing through the cabin. 'You're thinking of Luke Williams! You think that perhaps I used to meet him here. Is that it?'

'Did you?' he asked her with an edge to his tone.

'Of course not. You insult me. Do you know what Williams looked like?'

'I'm not interested.'

'No? But I'll tell you anyhow. He was a little runt of a man, dried up, older than Hugh. Del, I never met anyone like this before.'

Her voice had dropped to a whisper and she moved closer to him, and only then did he notice the flimsy thing she was wearing. His heart began pounding, and he felt her nearness, the softness of her body. His arms went about her, bruised her shoulders and back as she pulled his face down to her, meeting his mouth with kisses that sent wave after wave of exhilaration storming through him.

'Hold me tighter, Del. Please hold me...'

They were reeling across the cabin, locked in each other's arms, when a peal of thunder crashed through the stillness of the night. Another blast came, then another. Lory screamed, freeing herself.

'The dam! *They've blown up the dam!*'

Six

Pearce remained frozen until the last sonorous echoes of the explosions faded into silence. In the tense moment that followed he was besieged by a host of mixed feelings, vague stirrings of emotion that swept over him and left no lasting impression. One sensation crystallized, however, a quick surge of gladness that the dam had been wrecked. Lory sprang to the door and whipped the bar clear to spring outside.

Pearce watched her hurry to the bunkhouse where a commotion had already been triggered. He listened as the woman issued crisp orders, and soon shadowy forms were dashing towards the corral. He went to watch all this and then returned to the doorway of the cabin, where he was standing when Lory hurried back.

'Do you realize what they've done, what this means?' she cried.

He handed her the shawl. 'I told you his patience wouldn't last.' Oddly, he was incapable of feeling any sense of urgency.

Overacker had simply done what any red-blooded cowman would do. He had decided to fight when he had been pushed into a corner.

She was tugging at his arm, her fingers biting into his flesh. 'We'll have to stop them. We'll have to do something, Del.'

'It's a mite too late for that, I reckon.'

'Oh, damn you! You're taking it all so coolly. What has come over you? Aren't you going to ride up there with me?'

He moved past her without answering. He went to the corral, seeing the stragglers from the bunkhouse pounding after the leaders in the direction of the hills. He took a horse out and selected one for the woman. He saddled them both and brought them to the front of the main building. Lory had dashed inside, and now she emerged, wearing a heavy coat against the night chill. She thrust a rifle into the saddle-boot of the mount which Pearce held for her.

A yell from the window of Hugh Temple's room caused him to hold on, expecting Lory to go to speak to her husband.

'You'd better see him and explain what you're doing.'

'There's no time for that. Come on.'

It took a little while for him to overtake

90

her, and when he drew level she flung him a look before urging her horse to even greater speed. It required almost an hour for them to reach the new water-course and splash through. On the opposite bank, Lory halted to gesture frantically.

'That stream's running low already. They've managed to turn the water back into the river.'

Pearce made no comment. He followed her on to a loftier elevation, slowing when they hit rougher going. There were holes in the trail, sharp rocks where a horse could easily lose its footing and throw its rider. Lory paid no heed: she kept going, pushing her mount relentlessly, disregarding the danger.

Pearce reflected that this action of Overacker's, while entirely justifiable in his eyes, would almost certainly spark a shooting war between the two outfits. And Willa Overacker, that pretty niece of Leon's, would be caught in the middle of the whole dirty business.

The hills grew steeper, and at length they emerged on a bench of solid rock. Above them loomed the black, serrated peaks, and Pearce knew they were almost at the site of the dam. He dropped from the saddle and led his mount. Up above him, Lory was still pushing her horse, and he feared she might ruin the beast.

A rifle shot sounded off on their right; another one chimed in, this a fair distance away. Someone shouted, and then Pearce spotted a couple of men heading away across the skyline. Long T riders, he guessed, on the trail of the dam-blowers.

He soon heard a noisy gushing of water in full spate, and came over a section of rocks to see a thick curtain of spray turn to silver in the hard moonglow before dashing down the hillside, gathering momentum, while the din became a tremendous roar. Lory was off her horse now, standing on the lip of the great gash that had been blown in the rocks. Of the dam itself there was no trace. The whole rock shelving had been blown out, and now the river would teem into the distant river-bed that divided Split Diamond and Long T.

Lory was as rigid as the rocks themselves, set-lipped, staring out across the havoc that had been made of her carefully constructed plan.

A tall figure swung towards them out of the shadows, rifle at the ready. 'Is that you, Mrs Temple?'

'Burt!' She wheeled to him, and Pearce feared she would throw herself at the cow-hand. Burt took a hasty step backwards when Lory brought her own rifle curving up. 'Damn you. I've a good mind to shoot you where you stand,' she panted.

'Now take it easy, Mrs Temple,' the other protested. 'We did our best.'

'Easy!' she ranted. 'Tell me what happened. How did Overacker's men get so close to the dam? Why weren't you on the look-out?'

'You can't blame me,' the other retorted sourly. 'Nor Joe neither. These fellas snuck up on us in the dark. We were eating supper when they rushed us – four of them – and told us to freeze.'

'But the dynamite, damn it, Burt: how did they blow the dam?'

'They had a pack-horse. Two of them kept us covered while the others worked at set-ting the charge. They sure knew their jobs, too, the slick way they set it. When it was ready they took us away down the slope yonder. Ferraza showed up then, the damn fool. He walked right into their arms, calling our names.'

'So they set off the charge? Where are Joe and Jim now?'

'They went after the jaspers as soon as they

let us loose. I was scouting around here, trying to get a shot at them.'

'Did you recognize any of them?' the woman demanded next.

'Nope. They all had sacks over their heads, with holes for the eyes. But I know who they were all right.'

'Split Diamond?'

'Who else? And, Mrs Temple, if you'll pardon me saying it, I think the dam was a bad move in the first place.'

'I don't pay you to think,' she rounded icily on the cowhand. 'I pay you to do exactly as you're told.'

'Yes'm!' Burt grunted. He threw Pearce a probing look, but this was Lory's deal, and Pearce made no comment.

'Get after Joe and the others,' the woman ordered Burt. 'When you find them, tell them to report back to headquarters at once.'

'Sure thing, ma'am.'

Burt slouched off into a dark screen of brush. He emerged leading a horse and set off along the rocky slopes in the direction taken by the Split Diamond men and their pursuers. When he had disappeared, Lory moved over to the very edge of the crevice, peering away down at the boiling torrent of water. She joined Pearce after a few minutes.

'This doesn't appear to shock you at all, Del,' she said tersely.

'No, it doesn't surprise me. I'd have been more surprised if Overacker had sat back and let you walk all over him.'

'So you would have done things differently?'

'I might. Yes, I reckon I would, at that.'

'Very well then...' She made a little futile motion. 'So I've been a fool. I've been using a woman's psychology when it really required a man's ingenuity. What do you say, Pearce?' she ended challengingly. 'You're still my foreman?'

'Do you still want me to rod your outfit?' he countered.

'Of course.' Her tone hardened. 'We'll show that snake Overacker that we're not going to be beaten. We'll show him that he can't get away with such a dirty trick.'

'I figured you said I'd be giving the orders,' he reminded her.

'Have I said otherwise? You're in charge as from this minute. And the first thing you'll do is ride over to Split Diamond and show them that we really mean business.'

He tried to be patient with her. 'That's not what I had in mind.'

'You think we should burn them out then,

without any warning whatever?'

'I think you should let the river run as it's running right now, as it's been running all along, watering Split Diamond stuff as well as your own.'

'What! Are you crazy. I tell you I'm not letting them get away with it. I mean it, Del.'

'There's not much else you can do unless you really want a war.'

'If it's to be war, then well and good,' she panted. 'The sooner the better. If you're too scared to do it, then I'll do it myself.'

Before he could say anything more, much less argue with her, she had shaken out her mount's reins and was pushing it away from the raw rent in the rock formation. Pearce let her go. If her horse threw her and she broke her neck, then that would be just too bad.

He investigated the area for another thirty minutes or so before starting back to the Long T headquarters. He encountered no one on the journey, but when he rode into the front yard there were six or seven mounted men ranged in front of the house. Lory was holding forth.

'We're going to beard Overacker in his den right now,' she declared. 'We'll teach that old gopher a lesson he won't forget in a hurry.'

'What kind of lesson do you aim to teach him, ma'am?' someone asked anxiously. 'We can't just ride in there and shoot up the place without hearing Leon's side of the story. Maybe he didn't wreck the dam at all. The Bighorn feeds a few other outfits down south.'

'Sime,' the woman snapped at him, 'if you haven't got the sand to do what I tell you, then you can pack up and clear out.'

Pearce chose that moment to push his horse forward, and the woman switched her attention to him. 'I think you're making a big mistake,' he said quietly. 'Sime just raised a good point. Why not ask Overacker if he wrecked the dam?'

'Of course he did. There's no doubt about it.'

'Just the same, I think–'

'Pearce, it seems to me that you're not the tough customer my husband believed you to be.'

Someone chuckled at that and Pearce felt a tide of heat sweeping through his cheeks. He fought a surge of anger. 'Maybe so. But I'm inclined to believe you're going to start something you'll regret.'

'All right, Del,' she flung back. 'Stay where you are if you haven't the stomach for fighting our battles. Let's go, boys!'

She spurred away and the men followed her, moving out of the yard and soon disappearing into the darkness. Pearce sat his mount, heaving a sigh of resignation. What would happen to Willa Overacker now?

'Pearce, are you not going with Lory?'

He started at the voice, seeing a shadow at the window of Hugh Temple's lamp-lit room.

'Temple, it's a bad deal, and you know it. Why couldn't you make your wife see reason?'

The big man laughed, and the sound of it sent a chill dancing along Pearce's spine. 'You don't know that woman, mister. When she makes up her mind the devil himself couldn't turn her.'

'But she might get herself killed. Doesn't the idea worry you?'

'I know what you're thinking,' the other boomed. 'You figure I'm not overly concerned about her. Did it ever occur to you that I might know the kind of double-crossing little bitch she really is?'

Pearce could hardly believe his ears. He knew at that moment that Lory had lied to him about Luke Williams. Perhaps Temple guessed what had almost taken place over yonder in the foreman's cabin

'You talk mighty strange, Hugh. Anyhow, that's your affair, not mine. I don't care for fighting for its own sake.'

'You're worried about Leon Overacker.'

'His niece came home today. She's a nice kid. It's a hell of a homecoming, Hugh.'

'Then why don't you do something about it?' the rancher taunted. 'Go and warn Overacker. Maybe you really have lost your nerve, friend, huh?'

Pearce tried to make out Temple's features in the darkness, but it was impossible. He decided that he and his wife were well matched; they were both ruthless. They acknowledged nothing but their own over-riding ambitions. He reached a decision.

'I'm pulling out,' he told the cattleman. 'I'll see that you get your horse back shortly.'

'You'd be dead if I'd pulled out in Attica. Have you forgotten that?'

'I forget nothing. But you were a different man then. Maybe I can still find some way to repay you, a better way.'

Temple's harsh laugh grated on his nerves, caused a cold sweat to film his brow. For all he knew, the big man could have a gun lined on him.

He backed his horse away from the light of

the window. The mocking laughter followed him. 'Hell, Pearce, I'm not going to shoot you in the back.'

Pearce whirled the horse around and raked its flanks with his heels. In a short time the ranch buildings were behind him. He kept the beast to a punishing pace, taking the trail he was sure the Long T men would follow to reach Split Diamond. He had no real knowledge of the location of Overacker's headquarters, just a sketchy idea of the general direction in which the buckboard had been travelling earlier in the day. Even so, he must do his best to get there before Lory and her men.

He kept going for the better part of an hour. The moon was high in the heavens and its silvery light threw up patches of scrub timber and isolated clusters of sandstone in sharp relief. Soon he glimpsed shadows that appeared to be moving, and when he canted his head he was able to pick up the low drumming of racing hooves. He topped out a hill and descended into a sort of gloomy basin. Away off yonder at the bottom of the slope he discerned a glimmering of light and reined in, peering hard at the wall of darkness. If those lights marked the Split Diamond headquarters, then Lory and her crew must be there already and closing in on the ranch-house.

This slope of the basin had scatterings of thick brush and he went down it carefully, moving from one dense clump to another. He was dropping from the saddle to lead the sorrel the rest of the way when a man rose out of the ground in front of him. Pearce's right hand stabbed for his Colt, but a rifle barrel was already levelled on him.

'Freeze!' came a curt order.

Pearce lifted his arms and the man motioned with the rifle. 'See the light down there?'

'I see it.'

'Keep moving towards it. A bad move and you're dead.'

Still he hesitated, staring hard at the man in the hope of recognizing him. He was sure this wasn't a Temple rider. An Overacker man then? If so, how could he assure him that he wasn't an enemy?

'I was riding to warn your boss. This is Split Diamond country?'

'Answer to the first is, you're a liar. Second is, you're right. Who are you? One of Temple's bunch?'

'My name's Pearce. Del Pearce. I'd like to see–'

'Pearce, eh? The gunhawk that signed on with Long T? Well, well! I happen to know somebody who's just dying to see you, friend. Grab your horse's reins and get on down yonder. And no tricks.'

Pearce did as he was told, and when they drew close to the scattering of buildings another man stepped out. In spite of the darkness, Pearce recognized the foreman Grat who had visited Long T earlier in the day.

'Who is it, Rance?'

'Gent called Pearce, Grat. Found him spying around back there.'

'Pearce!' The foreman closed up and peered into the captive's face. 'So Lory sent you here on some dirty work?'

'You're wrong.'

'Ahuh! We'll soon see. Shuck your gunbelt.'

'Not till I see Overacker,' Pearce said doggedly.

He wasn't prepared for Grat swinging his fist. The blow caught him flush on the jaw and sent him reeling against the one called Rance. Pearce was setting himself to lunge at Grat when Rance jammed the bore of his rifle against his spine.

'Want me to blow a hole in you?'

Pearce breathed raggedly, glaring at the

foreman. He heard a door open and someone emerge on the porch. A girl spoke.

'Mr Jurado, what's the matter?'

'It's all right, Miss Willa. Rance found
some fella snooping around. You go back
inside, ma'am.'

But the girl stood where she was, peering
down at the newcomer. Pearce heard her
sharp intake of breath. 'Oh, it's you again!'

'Reckon so, Miss Willa.' Pearce grinned
wryly. 'I wanted to see your uncle.'

'But – but Uncle Leon said...'

'No matter what he said,' Pearce broke in.
'I came to warn you that there might be an
attack on the ranch. In fact, I'm sure there's
going to be one *pronto.*'

'A likely yarn,' Grat Jurado sneered. 'He's
up to no good, ma'am. He's a troublemaker,
a gunslinger. He's working for Lory Temple,
and she sent him here to–'

A rifle cracked flatly out there in the darkness and a heavy bullet ploughed into the
wall of the house. Willa Overacker screamed.
Another rifle opened up, this one from a
different angle. A window was smashed into
flying shards.

'Get inside,' Jurado roared at the girl.
'Pearce, this is part of your trick. You–'

Once more a burst of crimson rent the

darkness and Pearce heard the explosion on the instant something hot seared along his side and sent him spinning into the porch railing.

Willa Overacker screamed again, and Pearce heard her shout his name before he stumbled and fell. He was panting heavily and breathing was sheer agony. He made a desperate effort to grab a gallery rail for support, but his fingers slid back and his senses drifted away into a sea of blackness.

Seven

It was a strange sensation, living your life over again like this. Things were real and yet, somehow, they belonged to a dream world. Here he was, walking the streets of Carlsbad, with everything dark except for the saloon lamps cutting yellow swathes on the sidewalks. There was a big cowboy called McBane who had threatened to kill him for pistol-whipping his pard, and this McBane came out of an alley in front of him. The big fellow's eyes glittered insanely and the gun he held was a thing of flaming crimson. It spoke in Pearce's face, but he knew that his own revolver was in his hand, talking loudly, and that McBane was dead before he hit the plankwalk.

'Del Pearce,' the newspaper read, 'puts paid to another of the roughnecks who are threatening to destroy our town and our way of life. Pearce is well worth the money the town is paying him, and long may he reign!'

There was a woman called Kate, a blonde woman who worked in one of the saloons, and Kate was saying to him. *'You get out of here, Delbert, 'cause they're gunning for you...'* The use of that name always put him into stitches.

Again, a man was walking towards him down the street and calling him a yellow-belly, and he was telling the man to go home and sleep it off. This one wanted to shoot him, too – didn't they all – and he killed the man before he had his gun clear of leather. He laughed then and the sound of it ran through the town, and all the hardcases heard the challenge and came to take shots at him. He walked through them unscathed, and just as he reached the doorway of his office someone sniped at him from a high window across the street and he fell...

The shadows merged with other shadows. There was pain that came in hot flashes of agony and filled his whole being. He could hear voices in the distance at intervals. Something infinitely cool was being pressed against his forehead. He talked, trying to communicate with the people, and cursed when they persisted in remaining ghosts on the rim of his consciousness.

Finally, he opened his eyes and knew he was in a bed, and after a while it came to him that this was the headquarters of Leon Overacker's Split Diamond ranch. For good or ill, he had run out on Lory Temple.

'How do you feel now?' The voice was soft, concerned, not a strange voice, but one he had become familiar with in his dreams. He tried to bring the face into focus, and when he managed this he saw Willa Overacker smiling at him.

'I guess I – feel just fine...'

'Good! You must take it easy, though. The doctor says you must lie there and rest. No movement and no talking.'

'I see.' He lay back for a minute to gather his thoughts, then: 'Miss Willa, what happened?'

'Don't you remember? You were shot outside the ranch-house.'

'Heck, yes, I remember. Last night it was...'

'A week ago,' she said. 'But you mustn't talk about it. just rest.'

The door of the room opened and Leon Overacker came in. His steel-grey eyes flickered from his niece to the man on the bed. The eyes were expressionless.

'Can I talk to him, Willa?'

'Not yet, Uncle. He has just come round, as the doctor said he should. The fever has left him and he ought to get well soon.'

'The sooner the better. I don't aim to harbour any of that woman's crew for any longer than necessary.'

He was on his way out again when Pearce spoke weakly. 'Overacker, hold on a minute.'

'What is it?' The cattleman's features were hard, unyielding. 'You're not fit to talk yet,' he added brusquely. 'Later.' To Willa he said: 'Don't forget that he's a spy and means us no good.'

Pearce attempted to rise so that he could protest better; instead the strength left him suddenly and he slipped back into that dream world.

It was another week before he was able to sit up and feed himself. He knew that Willa Overacker had nursed him through his illness, and he had come to look on her as some kind of angel. She refused to talk about the night he had been shot, always saying that he was too weak to stand any excitement. But the day came when Pearce clutched her hand as she was about to leave the room.

'Willa, I've got to know what happened that night,' he pleaded.

'There is little to tell, really. Some men raided our ranch and began shooting. One of them shot you in the chest. Another inch in the wrong direction and you would have died.'

'Did – did they do any other harm?'

'None, apart from breaking windows. Uncle's boys opened fire on them and they soon turned tail.'

'And they haven't come back?'

She shook her head, studying him closely. 'I've heard a lot about you, Mr Pearce.'

'I bet you have! Call me, Del, won't you? I suppose your uncle has told you that I went to work for Lory Temple?'

'The woman who runs the Long T. Yes, and he won't believe that you came here to warn us of an attack. He is sure you meant us harm.'

'Has Mrs Temple ever come here?'

'Never, as far as I know.'

'I wonder if she knows I caught a bullet, if she knows I'm here,' he said half musingly.

'I believe she is a handsome woman.'

Pearce laughed shortly. 'Yeah, you could call her that, I guess. Say, when do you reckon I can get out of this bed, Willa? I feel pretty good again.'

'The doctor is due to visit tomorrow. He

will decide what you should do. But as I understand it, you won't be able to ride for a while.'

'Won't I? Well, you just hang around and see, young lady.'

'Del,' she said diffidently, 'would you do something for me, please?'

'Just name it, ma'am. I reckon I owe my life to you.'

'Nonsense. But would you have a talk with Uncle, tell him exactly what happened, and try to get him to see your side of the story?'

'All right,' he agreed after a moment's hesitation. 'But I don't think I'll make much headway. He has made his mind up about me.'

'But you *will* try?' she pressed eagerly and turned to the door. 'Can I tell him to come and see you now?'

'Why not? Say, Willa, do you think I could risk a smoke?'

'The doctor said no tobacco.'

'Just a couple of puffs,' he begged.

She relented then, full lips trembling in the effort she was making to keep from smiling. 'I'll get the makings from one of the boys.'

It was early evening before Leon Overacker

came into the room and stood at the end of the bed. The rancher was dressed in dusty riding garb and appeared to have been working hard. There was no warmth in his eyes as he said bluntly: 'I understand you want to see me.'

'That's right.' Now that he was here, Pearce found it difficult to make a start. 'First off, I want to thank you for keeping me here and allowing your niece to look after me.'

The rancher made an impatient gesture with his hand. 'I'd do it for anyone,' he said coldly. 'But I'll be glad to see you go, all the same.'

'I wouldn't be here at all if you hadn't blown up that dam,' Pearce reminded him. 'So you're partly responsible yourself.'

Overacker considered him for a few moments, and it seemed to Pearce that he was trying to reach some conclusion regarding him. 'The dam had to go,' he said. 'There was nothing else for it, other than declaring war on Long T. I would have taken that course, only Hugh was ill.'

'Was?' Pearce fastened on the word. 'You mean he's well again, able to leave that chair?'

Overacker hesitated, plainly turning something over in his mind. 'Willa hasn't told you then? But of course she wouldn't, seeing how ill you were.'

Pearce's puzzlement increased. There was something ominous behind the rancher's mood, his talk. His very manner grated on Pearce's nerves.

'Something *has* happened to Hugh? Maybe to Lory?'

'Hugh Temple is dead, mister.'

For a long minute Pearce could only stare at Overacker while he tried to comprehend the significance wrapped up in the stark words. Big Hugh Temple dead? It seemed impossible; it was utterly incredible.

'What – what happened?' he got out at last.

'He was shot,' the rancher replied evenly. 'The doctor tried to get him on to his feet a week ago. Hugh managed so well that he thought his back was cured, and maybe it was. Anyhow, he managed to get on to a buggy and travel to San Felipe with Sam Moro. Seems he was pretty all-in when he reached town. Moro took him into a saloon and got him a drink. Sam was at the counter when this stranger walked in – a stranger to San Felipe, that is. He walked right up to Temple and started cursing him some. Temple was heeled, and he must have lost

112

his head. Anyway, he went for his gun and this fella bored him clean.'

Pearce's heart was hammering madly by the time the recital was finished. A stranger had walked calmly into a saloon and shot Hugh Temple – just when it appeared that Hugh might be able to resume some kind of normal life? It meant that the stranger must have known Temple before he settled in the Bighorn Basin country. Could the stranger have been... But no, that was impossible.

'Did anyone get the name of this gunslinger?' he asked in a hoarse voice.

'He left the saloon right after the shooting,' Overacker explained. 'Somebody said it was the Tucson Kid.'

The shock caused Pearce to shrink back against his pillows, and for the first time a semblance of concern was reflected in Overacker's face.

'It seems to me that you might know this Kid: do you?'

Pearce sighed raggedly. 'Yes, I know him.'

'Then it figures. I was told that you and Temple had known each other before. He had saved your life or you had saved his. That was the reason for the mysterious abduction from the San Felipe stage. It meant you owed him something and he wanted to collect. Is that so?'

'Yeah, I owed him something all right. But Temple wasn't the kind to demand his pound of flesh. That was his wife's idea.'

'That figures as well. Mister, I don't know how you rate that woman, but as far as I'm concerned she's four kinds of hell-cat. Do you want to talk about it?'

Pearce shook his head. 'Not now. Look, Mr Overacker, I've got to get out of here. I've got to see Lory.'

'That's your business, of course. But I understand she's bearing up pretty well.'

Pearce ignored the underlying irony. 'Do you still believe that Hugh or his wife sent me down here to make trouble for you?'

'Guess I do, fella. Unless you can persuade me to the contrary.'

'Sorry, I don't feel up to it just now. Maybe later.'

'Suit yourself,' the other said. He turned to the door. 'Anyway, you can stay where you are until you're fit enough to travel.'

'Thanks, Overacker.'

Pearce sat staring at the wall for a long time after the rancher had left the room. That damned Tucson Kid again! He had hunted up Temple and settled his account with him. And that meant just one thing –

the Kid would have to settle his account with ex-lawman Delbert Pearce as well.

'I've got to get out of here...'

It was easier said than done. He managed to slip his feet to the floor and stand upright. He took a faltering step towards the door, and as luck would have it, the door swung open just then and Willa came in.

'Del Pearce, I never expected you to play such a trick on me!'

'But Willa, I was just trying. Darn it, I'll have to try.'

'Not yet you won't,' she scolded. 'Now straight back to bed. You must wait until the doctor tells you to get up.'

He returned to the bed obediently, but he was convinced that he would mend a lot quicker if only he could get out and about in the air and sunshine. 'I'm feeling a lot better,' he said. 'All thanks to you.'

The earnestness – and some other quality – in his voice caused her to avert her eyes, and now she was the shy creature of the stagecoach once more. He would really miss this girl when he rode away from Split Diamond eventually. There was small chance of her uncle extending an invitation for him to visit afterwards. Which, when everything was said and done, might be a good thing. His best course would probably be to move on out of the Bighorn Basin country after he had paid his respects to the Tucson Kid.

Her gaze moved slowly back to him and she misinterpreted his grave expression. 'Did – did you talk with Uncle?'

'Yes, I did. But it was no use. He'll never believe I'm anything else but a no-gooder.'

'Did you try explaining to him? Did you explain anything?'

'Explain? I might as well hammer my head on the ground.'

The girl stared glumly through the window for a few moments, then went out again. Pearce had sensed a change in her during that short time. There appeared to have been a subtle cooling of the warm intimacy that had developed between them, and he began to worry.

He had met many women in his time, the good ones and the not so good, but not until now had he met a girl quite like Willa Overacker. The future without her loomed as a colourless prospect.

Presently, he fell to wondering if Willa now shared some of her uncle's doubts concerning him. If that was the case, then his life would be scarcely worth living.

Eight

Lory Temple watched Sheriff Tom Neel from San Felipe lift his sparse frame into the saddle of his dun horse and ride off down the slope from the ranch-house. Then she went back to the gallery and sat down on her rocker, thinking over what the lawman had said.

'I'm still on the look-out for this Tucson Kid fella,' Neel had told her. 'I'd like you to get me word at once if any of your boys spot him about. I've a hunch he's mixed up in the beef-stealing that's going on, too.'

Lory had assured the grizzled star-packer that she would do that. The sheriff had been curious about Del Pearce, and had wanted to know more about him when she explained how Hugh had once helped Pearce get the better of the Kid in a town called Attica.

'Maybe this Pearce has some idea where the Kid hangs out,' Neel had said hopefully while he rubbed his stubbled chin. But Lory could tell him only that Pearce had stayed at the Long T for a day and then ridden off, never to be seen again.

Now, as the woman watched the lawman's form diminish on the flat below her, her thoughts settled on Pearce. What, she wondered, had happened that night when she led her crew out to throw a scare in Split Diamond? Pearce had stayed behind, but Lory had learnt from Hugh that the tall man had ridden out shortly after she did, and it had been Hugh's notion that Pearce had been headed for Split Diamond to warn Overacker of an attack.

She recalled how they had ridden to Overacker's place and fired on the house. Windows had been smashed but, as far as she understood, little other damage had been done. And when the Split Diamond men had commenced shooting back, the realization of what she had done hit her forcefully. Her men had been caught in the open without an experienced general, and been forced to flee in disarray. As things stood, the Bighorn still spilled across Split Diamond range and watered Overacker's stock, as it had always done. She had considered hiring expert engineers and building another dam, or dynamiting the rocks and letting the water run where it might as long as Split Diamond's supply was cut off. But Sam Moro had talked her out of that, warning her that she might deprive her own stock of the precious water.

Lory was coming out of the rocker when she noticed a rider approaching from the west. The horseman was moving at a brisk pace and riding directly towards the ranch buildings. Soon she recognized Jim Ferraza and frowned slightly. Since Hugh's death, Ferraza was growing bolder in his advances to her. He now addressed her as 'Lory', and the time had passed when she reminded him that she was to be called 'Boss' or 'Mrs Temple'. Ferraza was handsome after a fashion, and she feared the day would come when she would tire of resisting his overtures and yield to the man. It was something that always stayed on the edge of her mind, frightening her more than she was willing to admit.

Ferraza came in on a lathered horse, the bay stallion that had been the one Del Pearce had favoured, and slipped lithely to the ground. His face was shining from the use of a razor that morning. Ferraza shaved every day now, and Lory knew this was becoming a source of amusement in the bunkhouse. Already her name was being linked with the cowhand's, and when she had reinstated him as foreman and assigned him to the cabin at the back of the house, the other crew members were sure that Ferraza would soon make the conquest he desired.

'Lory, I just saw him down near Elk Creek,' was his gusty preamble. 'I knew damn well that gent would end up stabbing you in the back.'

Lory gaped at him for a moment, failing to comprehend the full import of the outburst. 'What on earth are you talking about, Jim?'

'That Pearce *hombre* that you licked up when he was here,' the other rejoined. 'I saw him with Overacker's niece. You know that little Willa thing, all brown hair and big eyes?'

Lory was aware of the blood leaving her face. She turned away from the foreman, not wanting him to see the pain that registered, the extent of the shock the news had given her. 'Are – are you sure it was Pearce?'

'No doubt about it. Large as life and ugly as sin.' Ferraza laughed and the sound rasped on her nerves.

'Stop it,' she cried fiercely when she could bear it no longer.

'But, Lory, I figured you should know. All this time he has been working for Over-acker. Are you forgetting that Hugh got himself killed because he helped Pearce out one time?'

Each word hammered the woman's sensibilities until her breathing became an agonized burning in her throat. Just then she looked like a stricken girl, innocent, defenceless, sorely in need of comfort and protection. Ferraza swallowed thickly and took a quick, involuntary step towards her, then placed a hand on her arm.

'Lory...'

She sprang at him like a wildcat, eyes flashing scornfully, her open hand cracking solidly against his face. Ferraza reeled back in astonishment.

'Damn it, you really were struck on him!' he accused.

'Leave me alone, damn you, Jim. I'll find out for myself, and if you've been lying to me you'll regret it.'

'But why should I lie?' he retorted.

'We'll see,' she said coldly. 'Go back to the crew, Jim. If Del Pearce has been working for Split Diamond all this time, and knows that Hugh was shot by the Tucson Kid, then I – I'll kill him myself.'

'You've been far too soft with that Split Diamond outfit,' Ferraza accused. 'Unless I miss my guess, it's old Leon who's stealing our stock.'

'You told me we were a hundred head down last month. Is that so?'

'It's the truth, and I'm sure Overacker's boys are doing the widelooping. Do you know what I'd do if I were in your boots?' Ferraza's tone was soft now, almost wheedling. A white weal had sprung up on his cheek and he touched it with gloved fingers.

'I know what you'd do,' Lory said bitterly. 'You think I should give him a dose of his own medicine and raid his stock.'

'Why not?' He was eager now, his cunning reasserting itself. 'If he's taking our beeves, we've the right to grab some of his. And you could easily sell them with the brands blotted over with a wet blanket and a running iron.'

Lory rounded on him. 'I'll have nothing to do with stealing, and don't mention such a thing to me again. Diverting the river was one thing – and my conscience was perfectly clear about it – but turning into a rogue is something else.'

Ferraza shrugged, looking sheepish. 'Whatever you say. I was just hoping our outfit had the guts to stand on its own legs for a change.'

'Leave it to me, Jim, please. And don't

repeat anything you've said to me.'

She turned into the house and Ferraza watched her go, her graceful stride striking little fires of desire in him so that he stood for a long time after she had gone from his view. He took the bay to the trough and pumped a drink, swilling the cold water over his face and head. He dried roughly with his bandanna and went into the saddle again, striking out for the western end of Long T graze.

The foreman rode through the sultry afternoon for an hour. Once he saw a couple of Temple men on the crest of a ridge, and reined in until they passed from out of sight. Then he moved off again, riding faster, as if the clock were set against him. Presently he came over a timbered ridge and hauled up where a couple of tall boulders dominated the area. He was rolling a cigarette when a horseman appeared behind him, causing him to start and grab for his gun.

'Hell, Kid, never do that on me!!' he complained to a thin, wiry, dark-skinned man of about forty. He wore chaps, black sombrero, and grey shirt. Two revolvers were thonged low at his sides.

The Tucson Kid bestowed a wintry smile on Ferraza. He had no time or inclination for indulging in pleasantries, and he flung a small sack which the foreman caught in mid-air.

'How does it feel?' the Tucson Kid said.

Ferraza opened the pouch and looked inside. His eyes sparkled and he nodded, grinning. 'Feels all right. Looks all right.'

'It should, friend. That stuff came all the way from California.'

'You figuring on going back there soon?' Ferraza wanted to know, double meaning in his words.

'I see plenty of good beef still in the Bighorn,' the Kid returned, lighting a cheroot.

'It's hellish hard to get it in the right place with so many Long T and Split Diamond riders about,' Ferraza reminded him.

'If it was easy, friend, you wouldn't be nursing that pouch of gold right now.' His tone became curt, businesslike. 'How many and how soon?'

Ferraza laughed nervously, but soon let the sound trickle away before the hard blue eyes that drilled into him. The Tucson Kid's humour – if he had ever possessed such a thing – had dried up long ago. Another thought occurred to Ferraza.

'I've seen Del Pearce,' he told the Kid, and watched interest quicken in the bleak eyes.

'When?'

'A few hours ago. He's working with Over-acker. Least, he was out riding with that Miss Willa.'

'Thanks for the news, friend. That one I want as well. He cost me four years of my life, him and Temple.'

'You got Temple.'

'I'll get Pearce too,' the Kid said thinly, memory churning hatred in him. 'Jim, there's some things I can't stand at all, mainly law-men, squealers and bunglers. Maybe you ought to remember that.'

'I won't forget,' Ferraza assured him, giving an involuntary shudder.

'When can you have the beef ready in the canyon?'

Ferraza considered, his fingers feeling through the canvas sack, greed shining in his face. 'Give me a week,' he said.

'I'll see you here a week from today.' The Tucson Kid nodded briefly and tugged at the reins of his spotted grey. He was mount-ing when Ferraza called to him.

'Kid, are you really going to do for Pearce?'

The dark-featured man regarded the foreman for a considerable time, his eyes calculating. 'You some friend of his?'

'Like blazes I am!' Ferraza chuckled. 'I tried to nail him myself the day he arrived on this range.'

'Then you won't mourn him, Jim.' And, so saying, the Tucson Kid pushed his horse in among the trees. The foliage rustled for a moment, glinted in the sunlight, then settled and was still, and there was no sound at all to mark the outlaw's trail.

Jim Ferraza mopped his sweaty forehead and felt the pouch of gold once more. He grinned and stuffed it away in a pocket. At this rate he would soon have a sizable hoard cached away. But it was hard work, all the same, and he earned everything he got. He would really need a helper to perform the task properly. But that would mean splitting the take, and it would mean letting someone know that he was betraying Long T.

The rider was silhouetted on the hill-top for only a minute, but even so, Del Pearce recognized him and brought the big sorrel he rode to a halt, staring up at the green summit where the horseman had vanished.

'Who was that man, Del?'

'A Long T rider,' he answered slowly. 'Name of Jim Ferraza.'

'I know Ferraza,' Willa Overacker said.

'Uncle Leon told me he heard he had been arrested up north for cattle stealing. The sheriff was unable to make the charge brought by a rancher stick.'

'You don't say!' The news surprised Pearce in a way; in another way it was probably something to be expected of a man like Jim Ferraza. 'Well, your uncle could be right. But he spotted me for sure, and he'll tell Lory where I am.'

'I'm sure she wondered why you never went back there.'

Pearce nodded, his eyes clouding. The past few days had been among the happiest of Pearce's life. Willa had taken him for short rides at first, to let him get the feel of a saddle under him again. Each day their rides had taken them further from Split Diamond headquarters. He knew that Leon Overacker frowned on his niece's interest in him, but he gradually came to realize that the rancher trusted him after all.

Each day he grew stronger, and he knew the time must come soon when he would ride away from Overacker's ranch and this lovely girl, and seek out the Tucson Kid.

'I'll have to see her, I guess,' he replied to Willa's question. 'Your uncle told me about Hugh's death, the way he was killed, I mean.'

127

Willa sighed and her head drooped. 'Yes, I knew you would find out sooner or later. Hugh Temple did you a favour once that earned the hatred of the Tucson Kid.'

'That's the size of it, I reckon. I'll just have to even for Hugh.'

'But, Del, you're not thinking of going after that man to – to try and kill him?'

He wilted under the challenging fire in her eyes. 'There are some things a man can't avoid doing.'

Later that same day, Leon Overacker came to him where he sat at the back of the barn, and surprised him cleaning his revolver. Since coming to Split Diamond, Pearce had not worn his gun-belt; now it was buckled around his waist and he was making sure the Colt was in first-class working order.

'Pearce, Willa tells me you might be heading out soon. Is it true?'

'I reckon.' He found it hard to meet the cowman's penetrating gaze. 'I guess I'm about fit enough to make my own way. I'll always be grateful to you, but I can't impose on you any longer.'

The older man sighed and perched on the edge of a chair. He fished out a pipe, tamped the dottle down in the bowl. 'I've been hasty with you, Pearce. Hasty in my judgement. I want you to know that my opinion of you has changed a mite.'

'Thanks, Overacker. That's handsome of you.'

The rancher paused for the time it took to strike a match and get his pipe going. 'There's something else I'd like to say to you. There's a berth here for you if you'll forget about this Tucson Kid and go to work punching cows for me. Grat has told me that Long T is missing cattle, just as we are. He thinks an organized gang of wideloopers are working the Bighorn country, and they might get around to making bigger steals. We all know by now you used to be a lawman. That makes you someone I wouldn't mind having on my payroll.'

It was a tempting offer, to be sure, and the fact that he would be near Willa made it all the more appealing. Still, Pearce shook his head after thinking it over. 'Thanks all the same. But I've got a private chore to do before I can settle down anywhere.'

'You've really made up your mind to leave then?'

'I have. I'd like to pull my freight first thing in the morning.'

'Just as you say.' The warmth went out of

the rancher's eyes and he nodded coolly. He went back round the corner of the barn, and soon Pearce heard him talking with one of the men.

Pearce put his gun away and lifted his gaze to the grey line of hills that marched across the sky in the distance. He began to think of Lory Temple, and wondered how the woman would react when he rode into her front yard again.

Nine

Del Pearce crossed the Bighorn early next morning and entered Long T graze. He travelled in a leisurely manner, not wanting to reach ranch headquarters until the crew had ridden out for the day. Still, he was anxious to see Lory before she had a chance to ride off somewhere.

Drawing closer to the ranch-house, he slowed, and when he was in full view of the long front gallery he hauled up, seeing a man at the corner of the house with a rifle at the ready. No second look was required to tell Pearce that this was Jim Ferraza, and he experienced a prickle of anxiety. What if Lory had given orders to shoot him on sight?

'That's about near enough, mister!' Ferraza called. Excitement pulsed in his voice, eagerness, and Pearce grated his teeth.

'Put that damn gun up,' he said coldly.

'Not on your life, friend Pearce. Now, just turn around and get out of here. You're on the skunk list as far as this outfit's concerned.'

'So you're the boss now, huh?'

'Just about.' Ferraza smiled sardonically. 'The right man for the job.'

Pearce looked on past him, seeing how the Chinese cook had come to the end of the bunkhouse to peep out. Astonishment came to his face and he turned tail quickly and vanished.

'You heard me, skunk. Get moving.'

'Where's Mrs Temple?' Pearce countered.

'None of your business. Get the hell off'n this spread.'

The rifle came up to Ferraza's shoulder and he lined the newcomer in his sights. At that moment something in dark blue showed at the end of the bunkhouse and Pearce swung to see Lory Temple.

'Jim, where is—' She broke off and appeared to freeze.

The dress she wore was full-skirted and cut low at the neck. Her dark hair was caught up in a coil at the top of her head, and for an instant Pearce had a vivid memory of this woman in his arms. He edged the sorrel towards her and Jim Ferraza called harsh warning.

'I done told you, mister! I'll shoot.'

'Howdy, Lory,' Pearce murmured, looking down at her.

She had gone pale at the sight of him, and just then her eyes appeared haunted with some painful memory of her own. Then fire swept through the paleness and the regard she put on Pearce was hot with scorn and hatred.

'You heard what Jim said.'

'I'll talk to Jim later,' he responded roughly. 'Right now I want to talk to you.'

'I don't wish to talk. I don't wish to listen to you.'

'I think you *will* listen to me, Lory. Take a good look at me and see if you notice any change in the jasper you brought on to this range.'

Her eyes were running over him as he spoke, without the injunction. Puzzlement was mirrored in her face, a kind of wonderment. He knew he looked peaked and that he had lost weight. She was taking note of all this and trying to guess at the reason.

'What – what happened to you?' she got out at length.

'One of your boys shot me that night. I've been sick since.'

'What! But Jim told me...' She swung to the rangy man who was staring bleakly at them. Ferraza said nothing.

'I saw Jim,' Pearce told her. 'He was

133

snooping on Split Diamond graze. Lory, tell me something before we go any further: have you put a wide loop in your rope?'

She fell back with a gasp. 'You're accusing me of rustling?'

'Let me take care of him,' Ferraza suggested.

'Be quiet,' she snapped at him. Her eyes drilled into Pearce. 'Come to the house with me,' she ordered.

Ferraza started to object, but an angry motion caused him to break off. Pearce hitched the sorrel to a rail and the foreman moved in closer to examine the horse.

'That's one of our string you've got there,' he accused.

'I brought it back,' Pearce said patiently. 'I couldn't get here any sooner.'

'I just bet you couldn't. You were too busy riding around with that Willa–'

He was close to Pearce when he said that, and Pearce chopped the edge of his right hand against his cheek. Ferraza fell back, cursing, trying to bring the rifle up. Pearce buried his right fist in the man's midriff, feeling an excruciating pain in his side and chest. Ferraza stumbled and went down, and before he could get up, Pearce smashed his knee into the angle of the cowhand's jaw, putting him down again like a felled steer.

Lory clutched Pearce's arm, but he brushed her off. 'He needs a lesson pretty bad.'

Ferraza came slowly to his knees. Blood trickled from a cut on his cheek. He appeared to be dazed and shook his head from side to side. When he was able to focus properly he found himself looking down the barrel of Pearce's .45.

'Next time you see this in my hand you'll be one second from hell, Jim,' Pearce told him. 'And that'll happen when you speak Miss Overacker's name again in my presence. Get it?'

Ferraza made no reply. Just coughed a couple of times and tried to control the sickness that gripped him. Lory had gone on to the house and Pearce followed her, holstering his gun when he reached the doorway and saw Ferraza still on the ground.

Lory ushered him through to Hugh Temple's room, and Pearce could almost feel the presence of the big man. The empty chair was pushed into a corner, close to the window. The telescope lay on a table nearby.

'I'm really sorry,' he said lamely.

'About Hugh?' There was weariness in her voice. 'Well, I suppose you should be. He was killed partly on account of you, after all.'

'I only heard a short time ago. I was pretty ill. I knew nothing for a week or so. Whoever fired at me nearly finished me off.'

'You left that night to warn them,' she accused.

'Because I didn't want bloodshed, damn it.'

'Do you know this Tucson Kid? I understand that you do.'

'I know him all right. Hugh told you the story, didn't he? Ferraza has heard it, too, by the sound of him.'

'Everyone knows it,' she said. 'Including the sheriff in San Felipe.'

She produced a whisky bottle and extended it, but he shook his head.

'Is Jim the foreman as before?'

'For the time being. You said something about rustling...'

'I wondered if you'd turned to cattle-stealing, just for the devil of it.'

'You insult me, Del. You're pretty good at throwing insults at me. But somebody is certainly in the rustling game. I've lost about a hundred head myself.'

'You have?' Pearce frowned. 'Lory, this might surprise you, but I've heard hints about Jim. You don't think–'

'Jim is sure that Overacker is stealing from us,' she broke in steadily. 'How do I know that he isn't, and trying to blacken Jim's name at the same time?'

'You don't know, of course. But I can tell you that Leon Overacker would never stoop to rustling.'

'So you know him pretty well?' Her lips bent in a little sneer. 'Maybe you know almost as much about his niece?'

'Willa is a good, sweet–' He broke off quickly, heat storming through his face, realizing too late that he had walked into a trap.

The woman's eyes glittered with blatant jealousy. 'Good and sweet? Well, isn't that just nice! I suppose she held your hand all the time you were ill, and told you fairy tales to put you to sleep at night?'

'Stop it, Lory!'

'I'll not stop,' she retorted. She moved closer to him, her nostrils dilating. 'Listen, Del, my husband was back on his feet. He was able to walk a little, ride a little. In a few more months he could have been back in control here. Now he's dead. *He was killed because of you, damn it!*'

'You don't have to hammer the point home.'

'I'll hammer it home all right. What's more, I'm going to keep you here until Long T is the ranch I want it to be. You're going to help me.'

'Wait a minute,' he objected. 'You've got it all wrong. I called to say I'm sorry and to return the sorrel, or pay for it, as I'd like to do. Then I'm going to hunt up the Tucson Kid. When I take care of him my life will be my own again.'

'But I need you here. Please, Del ... I – I thought we'd come to an understanding. Tell me it still holds.'

'No, it doesn't,' he said hoarsely. 'It just wouldn't work out. You're boss of this outfit, and any foreman you'd appoint would only be a puppet. You'd always have to hold the strings, Lory.'

'No, you're wrong,' she protested vehemently. 'This time it'll be different. I promise you it will be different.'

'Yeah?' His eyes glittered like pieces of ice. 'At least, Hugh won't be around to shoot any more of your lovers.'

She blanched, sucking a hard breath through her teeth. 'You're thinking of Luke Williams again?'

'I heard him mentioned over at the Split Diamond,' he told her. 'Seems he was a big gent too, almost as big as Hugh. And they say he had quite a way with women.'

A shudder ran through her and she closed her eyes momentarily. Then: 'All right, Del, so I told you a lie about Luke. But only about his appearance. There was nothing at all between us.'

'If that's the case, then I bet it wasn't your fault, Lory.'

She hit him then, and he might have expected that she would. It was a hard, stinging blow that slapped his head sideways. 'Get out of here,' she hissed. 'Get out before I have Jim shoot you. He's dying to put a bullet into you.'

'I'm going,' he said calmly. 'Not because I'm afraid of Jim. But before I go I want to pay you for that sorrel.'

'The horse is yours, damn you. Take it. I wouldn't touch a cent of your money, Pearce. And I only hope the Tucson Kid kills you, just as he killed Hugh.'

He inclined his head slightly, wheeled to leave the room. Her sobbing brought him swinging around in the doorway, and for a second something like remorse showed in his face. Then he shrugged and went on out. He was climbing aboard the sorrel when the woman emerged from the house.

'While you're about it, you can tell Overacker that I'm not through with him,' she cried. 'I'm going to teach him to keep his hands off my water.'

'You're losing cattle, Lory. I'd advise you to concentrate on finding out who's stealing your beef. Overacker is a straight rancher, and he wants no trouble. And, just in case Hugh didn't tell you, the Tucson Kid is a cattle rustler. It's possible he's operating in these parts.'

'I hope he kills you,' she raged.

He lifted his hand in a brief salute and gigged the sorrel away from the house. He looked around for sign of Ferraza, but the cowhand was not to be seen, and he rode on quickly in case Ferraza would be tempted to take a long shot at him.

He had almost reached the fork where the trail joined the San Felipe road when he heard hoofbeats hammering in his rear. He eased in and turned about, watching a rider pounding towards him. At first he thought it might be Jim Ferraza again, but then he saw that this rider was much shorter than Ferraza and much bulkier in the saddle. Presently he was able to make out the blunt features of Sam Moro.

By the time the cowhand had reined in

Pearce's .45 was already in his hand and resting on the saddle-horn. The Long T rider looked grim and angry.

'You can put that gun away, Pearce,' he cried breathlessly. 'I'm not on a hunting trip.'

'What's on your mind then, Sam?'

'Jim told me you'd come back,' the other replied, still breathing heavily from his hard exertion. 'I figured that maybe you were going to take over from that damn upstart.'

'Say, do you happen to be talking about your pard, Jim?'

'Who else? And he's no pard of mine, mister. As a matter of fact, I happen to be keeping a close eye on him.'

Pearce emitted a low whistle. 'Is he making up to Lory, smuggling snakes into the bunkhouse?'

'He's making up to the boss right enough, but who cares? Pearce, I reckon I must tell you something: I'm sure he's helping to steal our cattle.'

Pearce's expression underwent a rapid change. The wry amusement left his features and his eyes narrowed to pinpoints. 'That's a hefty charge to make against a man, Sam. Can you back it up?'

'I can't swear it's true, but a couple of the

141

boys say they've seen Jim riding out to meet a couple of strangers from time to time.'

'Well, by golly, imagine that! Sam, do you know the Tucson Kid?'

'I was with Hugh when that hellion killed him,' Moro revealed. 'But it happened so quick there was nothing I could do about it. I just heard this jasper calling Hugh a lot of dirty names, and then he drew his gun. Before the smoke had rightly settled he was through the saloon door and away on his horse. You're going after him, ain't you?'

Pearce nodded. 'The Kid used to have a fondness for other folks' cattle, Sam, and it's just possible that he's working this range.'

'Hold on, Pearce, you don't reckon that Jim is—'

'You maybe know that better than I do,' Pearce interrupted him. 'But I wouldn't ask Ferraza about the Kid if I were you. Just go easy and keep an eye on him.'

'I'm already doing that,' was the grim response. 'But, Pearce, you left Lory crying. I saw her. She couldn't speak for crying. You hurt her.'

'Never meant to hurt her, Sam. She wanted me to stay at Long T, and I told her I've got other things to do.'

'I see.' Moro scrubbed his stubbled chin

with the back of his hand. 'You got shot that night at Overacker's place, didn't you?'

'You're right there. Somebody figured a lump of lead would make me look real cute. Say, maybe you know who tried to bore me?'

Moro nodded. 'I just might, at that. I hate ambushers and back-stabbers.'

'No more than I do, pard. So the gent who planted the slug in me could have been you?'

Moro laughed shortly, spitting through his horse's ears. 'Could have been. But how can a man tell who he's shooting at in the dark?'

'Yeah, maybe you're right.' Pearce made a gesture with his gun. 'I'll let you move off first, mister.'

'Don't worry, Pearce. I don't make a practice of bushwhacking. But look out when you run into this Tucson Kid.'

'Thanks for the tip,' Pearce rejoined drily.

He waited while Sam Moro pulled his horse around and set off in the direction of the Long T headquarters, then he holstered his gun and pushed the sorrel towards the San Felipe road.

Once again he found himself thinking of the man who had fired at him when he had been travelling to the dam with Lory. Could that have been Sam Moro rather than Jim Ferraza?

'Sam's certainly a queer joker,' he mused. 'And he's sure worth keeping a close eye on.' Another thought occurred to him that caused him to chuckle. 'Say, that Sam bird wouldn't fancy moving into Lory's private quarters, would he? But why not? A man never knows, does he?'

One thing was certain, however: Lory Temple could have her pick of the range if she wanted a man to take Hugh's place.

Ten

The town of San Felipe turned out to be a lot bigger than Pearce had imagined it would be. There was a veritable network of streets and alleys, all criss-crossing, all dusty and fronted with buildings of every shape and size. No two buildings were uniform in construction, no two were alike in any respect. Here was a sizable, brick-faced edifice, there a dilapidated frame structure, apparently on the point of collapse. Paint seemed to be at a premium and glass an evident luxury.

At the head of the main street was a disused stamp mill that had once pounded out a steady rhythm in its pursuit of silver. But the mines that put the town on the map had long since closed and the mill had been a long time silent. Yet evidence remained of the former boom-camp style of living in the tar-paper shanties that clung to the hillside and the bleached, mildewed canvas strips that trailed forlornly from broken rails and struts along the river bank. The main volume of the Bighorn thundered through the

145

town each spring, when the snows melted, but thereafter, throughout the rest of the year, it was a shallow, lazy water-course which the citizens took for granted.

When the pay-dirt had petered out, San Felipe became a cowtown, catering for the needs of the newly-established cattle outfits and, later, for the influx of dirt farmers. Now the past persisted in clinging to the present to give an impression of incongruous gaudy finery in the midst of grey, drab desolation.

Pearce spent the better part of an hour viewing the town after he had put the sorrel up in the livery. He ate a meal in a restaurant and then went in search of the law-office, rubbing shoulders with booted and spurred cattlemen, stolid, dark-faced farmers, and Mexican *vaqueros* in colourful serapes and high-crowned, peaked sombreros. He found the sheriff's quarters down a side street where a sign proclaimed that the area was called Fourth Avenue, and went inside.

The elderly lawman was engaged in some paper-work, and he continued to scrawl laboriously with a pen that left little blobs of ink here and there on the paper. Pearce waited patiently until he had finished writing and signed his name with a flourish that required more practice. Then he cleared his throat noisily and the sheriff looked up, showing wonderfully clear blue eyes lurking beneath thick, shaggy brows. The eyes ran over the newcomer, making swift, expert appraisal.

'Howdy,' he said. 'I reckon you're Delbert Pearce.' He grinned meagrely at Pearce's surprise. 'I've heard all about you, Pearce, and I've been expecting a visit since Hugh Temple got himself killed in the Greenhorn. You've been away somewhere?'

'I've been staying at Overacker's Split Diamond for a spell,' Pearce returned cryptically. 'I haven't been doing a lot of riding recently.'

'I see.' If Tom Neel was interested in that aspect of his affairs, he pressed for no other information. 'And now that you're doing a piece of riding again you're looking for the Tucson Kid?'

Pearce ignored the obvious sarcasm. He nodded. 'That's the size of it, I guess. Can you tell me anything at all about him?'

'Not a great deal.' Neel drummed his blunt fingers on the desk. 'The Kid cleared town pretty *pronto* after he drilled Temple. The killing took everybody flatfooted. I was rather hoping that you might be able to tell

147

me something about him, where he might be hanging out, I mean.'

'You don't know if he's got any cronies here in town?'

'If he has I've never heard of them,' Neel replied. 'From what I gather, the Kid is a fly-by-night, here today and fifty miles away tomorrow.'

'I guess you're right, Sheriff. Thanks anyhow.' Pearce turned to the door and the lawman spoke after him.

'You didn't come to any harm when you got that sudden invite to quit the stage?'

Pearce chuckled. 'So you heard about that as well? No, nothing that I couldn't get over.'

'You're not making any charges then? Willa Overacker told me about it after the crew had reported. She was mighty worried about you.'

'Everything's fine now, Sheriff,' Pearce assured him. He left the office before the lawman could think of something else to ask him.

He spent most of the day in making the rounds of the saloons. He made discreet inquiries about the Tucson Kid, but everywhere he was met with blank stares or the shake of a head and a murmured apology.

148

Nobody had seen the Tucson Kid. Nobody appeared even to have heard of the Tucson Kid. In short, no one wanted to talk about the outlaw.

At nightfall, feeling the strain of so much exertion so soon after his illness, he booked a room at a hotel and turned in. He slept right through until midmorning and ate a hearty breakfast in the dining-room. He made several purchases at stores before going on to collect his horse. He was bringing the sorrel out of the livery when a skinny man wearing a stovepipe hat and ragged black coat accosted him.

'Excuse me, are you Mr Pearce?'

Pearce was amazed to discover he could be recognized in this town and he went on guard at once. He said tautly. 'That's right. What about it?'

'I heard talk that you were looking for the man who shot Hugh Temple, Mr Pearce. Hugh and you were pards, weren't you?' That was accompanied by an ingratiating smile and Pearce nodded.

'Maybe,' he conceded. 'Say, do you happen to know the Tucson Kid?'

'Well, I have to admit that I've seen him.' The man threw an anxious glance at the livery, then said in a whisper: 'I've seen him in town.'

'You have? When? Where?'

'Mr Pearce, you haven't got a couple of bits you don't need?'

'Reckon I'm right out of *dinero*, pard.' Pearce stuck his boot into the stirrup and levered himself to the sorrel's saddle.

'Say, hold on! Do you not want to hear me out?'

'You can't tell me anything, Jack.'

'It might help if you knew who the Kid was with.'

That made Pearce haul on his reins. 'Now lookit,' he said gently. 'I've no time for tall tales. If it's worth two bits I'll give you half a dollar. If it ain't, then I won't.'

The man shrugged. He had probably known better days. He fingered the tip of his nose. 'You know the Long T spread run by a woman – Hugh Temple's outfit?'

Excitement lifted in Pearce immediately, but he concealed it effectively. 'Yeah, I know the outfit you're talking about.'

'You know Jim Ferraza?'

'You're saying you saw Ferraza with the Tucson Kid?'

'You figured I was bluffing, didn't you?' the other sneered. 'I saw them right in this town, mister. Thick as... Damn it, I was just going to say thieves. I saw them go into the back room at the Golden Eagle. They stayed long enough to tell family histories. That ain't worth fifty cents?'

'It's worth a whole dollar, friend.' Pearce searched for the money and handed it over. Before the man could hurry away he said: 'What's your name, by the way?'

'Uh-uh! Never mind the name thing. I don't want to have to go around wearing a slug in my back.'

'Don't be a damn fool. I'm not going to put a rope round your throat. You could earn more money if you keep your ear to the ground. I want the Kid real bad, and I bet you know that damn well. Absolutely no come-backs.'

The man thought that over. 'When will you be in town again?'

'Heck, I don't know. Some time, I'm sure, if I don't run the Kid to earth first.'

'All right, Mr Pearce. I'm Cy Ford, and you can usually find me in the Golden Eagle. Right near the end of Main on this side.'

Pearce nodded. 'Thanks a heap, Ford.' He pushed the sorrel on through the dust.

He knew a relief when he was out on the

open plains. He had spent so much time in towns like Attica that he had come to associate any two rows of buildings with tension and violence. He had no desire to be a lawman again, felt he would never wear a badge at any price, and of a sudden he had a yearning to go back to John Halley's Triple X and get to punching cattle once more. First off, though, he had to settle accounts with the Tucson Kid.

Cy Ford's news had given him something to go on. Sam Moro suspected Jim Ferraza of being in cahoots with the beef-stealers, as did some of the Split Diamond crew, and now he had learnt that the foreman had been seen in San Felipe with the Tucson Kid. Which seemed to point to the Kid being at work on these cattle ranges.

Lory Temple should know of Ferraza's deceit, but if he revealed the cowboy's activities to Lory it would almost certainly spell disaster to his hopes of finding the Tucson Kid. No, the thing to do was scout around and find out what he could about the Kid's movements.

He rode back leisurely along the wagon road that forked off on one side to the Split Diamond and on the other to Long T. When he reached the signboard he halted and smoked a cigarette while he debated on the wisdom of warning Leon Overacker. This brought him to thinking of Willa, and he dismissed the notion, believing that it might be unwise to see the girl just now.

He moved on around the Long T headquarters, giving the ranch buildings a wide berth, but pausing on a hill-top to survey the place briefly before pushing deeper into the hills. He had bought supplies and a new tarp, and was thus well equipped for spending a few days out of doors. The air on this high range would prove beneficial and the exercise would help him regain his strength and stamina.

Here and there he came on grassy pockets in the rocks where some of the Long T stuff had strayed, and he wondered if Lory's men had a tally on them. There were numerous small streams curling out of the higher hills, and he thought it strange that Lory should ever have considered diverting the river. He could only conclude that the woman wanted to force Leon Overacker right off this end of the range.

In a cleft in the hills, Pearce came on the remains of a camp-fire and spent some time looking the place over, trying to decide whether Long T men had camped there or if there was the possibility that it had been a hide-out for the Tucson Kid. There was no sign of cattle, and this tended to bear out the latter surmise. Excited now, Pearce settled down to scout the country properly. It might take days to come across the Kid if he really was working this range. But Pearce was in no hurry; he was certain that, sooner or later, he would come face to face with the man who had killed Hugh Temple and who was likely planning at this very minute how he could get the former marshal of Attica lined up in his sights.

Lory Temple twisted and turned in her bed. A pale moon sailed aloft, and its light lanced through an opening in the curtains and fell across her face, like ghostly fingers almost. She thought of her late husband Hugh and shivered slightly. The house was too big for one person, especially at night, when boards creaked in the cooling air and caused her to imagine stealthy footsteps in the hallway.

The moon rode out until its radiance filled the room with cold, silvery light, and Lory rose presently and went to the window, thinking to draw the curtains closer. From here she could see the cabin where Jim Ferraza slept, and she stood for a while, thinking of Ferraza, thinking of Del Pearce knocking Jim down because he had spoken Willa Overacker's name. A wave of jealousy swept over her and she bit her underlip, wishing Willa Overacker had stayed away from the Bighorn Basin, wishing that Del Pearce were here on the Long T to stand by her, help her make the ranch the hub of the cattle empire she had dreamed of. Where was Pearce now? Was he on some lonely trail, trying to find the killer of her husband?

She was turning away from the window when something caught her eye over at Ferraza's cabin. Someone had come to the doorway, and she recognized her foreman. Ferraza was fully dressed and had his hat slanted over his face. He paused for a moment in the moonglow, glancing around him, and Lory knew when he was concentrating on her window. She stood back in case he might see her silhouette, wondering what he had in mind. She watched closely as Ferraza stepped away from the cabin, soon vanishing into the shadows.

Lory closed the curtains and frowned. She consulted a watch that had been Hugh's and saw that it had just gone one o'clock. Where could Ferraza be going at this hour? For a moment Lory debated with herself and

155

then, reaching a decision, she began to dress quickly, choosing a thick blouse and whip-cord riding skirt. When she finally slipped from the front of the house she had a wide-brimmed sombrero tugged down on her dark head. She paused in the shadows of the gallery, glancing towards the stable. Had Jim gone in that direction, as she suspected he had?

She heard a horse coming out then, its hooves making little noise. The rider was Ferraza, and he turned away across the front yard at a walk, angled down the slope leading to the open range, and soon dis-appeared.

Lory hurried to the corral and brought out her favourite pony. She saddled swiftly, try-ing to make up her mind whether she should bring Sam Moro along. She decided to fol-low her foreman alone. Sam might wonder at her anxiety over Ferraza. He might laugh at her and say Jim was likely heading off to see some girl.

At the bottom of the slope, Lory halted the pony in order to fix the direction of Ferraza's travel in her mind. She heard hoofbeats up ahead, moving fast now in the direction of the Bighorn, and she pushed her mount on, judging that Ferraza was either making for the town road or intending to cross the river and enter Split Diamond land.

The idea of her foreman riding for Overacker's place chilled her, and now she recalled Del Pearce asking her if she had a wide loop in her rope. Was it possible that Jim was heading off on a one-man rustling foray?

She slowed when she drew near to the river, peering ahead to try and distinguish shapes in the wan moonlight. She fancied she heard a horse splashing through at the ford and held back, not wanting to draw too close to the foreman. She thought of Ferraza now as somehow sinister, somehow dangerous. She had no way of telling how he would react if he discovered she was trailing him.

There was no sign of the cowhand at the ford, and the noisy flow of the water prevented her hearing anything else. But there seemed no doubt that Ferraza was cutting through Split Diamond graze.

A hill loomed ahead and she caught her breath when she glimpsed a horseman outlined against the starry sky. He remained there for a mere instant before disappearing over the ridge. Ferraza, without doubt. The night was chill, with a grey mist filtering through the grassy hollows, and Lory was glad she had donned warm clothing. When she crested the rise she halted once more and caught a glimpse of a shadowy form making its way towards the northern section of Overacker's territory.

A half-hour went past, with the cold becoming more pronounced. Cattle sprawled here and there in small bunches, and she began to worry about encountering a Split Diamond nighthawk. The country grew rougher and the groups of cattle more numerous. Then Lory heard a cow lowing plaintively and another joining in. She was soon able to make out a small herd of stock up ahead. The animals were on the move, perhaps a dozen all told, and there was no doubt that someone was rousing them and coaxing them into motion.

Lory held her breath, straining her eyes to catch sight of the herder. She heard a man call gruffly, heard a dull, slapping sound. And then she saw him. He was moving around the edge of the herd, swinging the animals into lumbering movement towards the north.

Lory sat still for a while, frozen with dread, scarcely able to believe the evidence of her eyes. That the herder was her foreman, Jim Ferraza, she had no doubt whatever. But the very boldness of the man took her breath away. What would happen now should some of Leon Overacker's men come on the scene? What would happen if they found Lory Temple, the rustler's boss, here as well?

Realization of the terrible danger she was in filled her with panic, and she was just about to swing her pony around when the rider with the cattle broke away and called in a low, anxious voice.

'Who's that?'

Lory was petrified now. If she made a move, Ferraza might open fire on her. If he did so, the shooting would attract any night riders in the vicinity. Yet she could not stay here and let Ferraza find out that she had been trailing him since he left headquarters.

He called again. 'Who's there?' The challenge was sharper, more fearful, and more likely to result in a bullet being fired unless it was answered satisfactorily.

Lory tried to make her tongue form words. She failed. And then her limbs seemed to come alive again. She wheeled her pony around and drove her heels into its sides, sending it tearing through the grass, heedless of direction as long as she got away from her foreman before he could discover her identity.

She feared that, at any second, a gun would bark and a bullet would catch her in the back. She had seen what a revolver bullet could do to a man, and her blood ran cold as she urged the pony to greater effort. She soon heard Ferraza's horse coming in pursuit, and she flailed herself for a fool. Had she kept her nerve back there and held her ground Ferraza would likely have taken cold feet and ridden off, thinking she was a Split Diamond rider. As it was, he had taken courage and was determined now to find out who had been trailing him.

Lory reached the end of a lope and saw a tangle of scrub timber over on her left. She angled into that direction, hoping to shake the man off, and hoping, too, that he would decide to make his getaway while the going was good.

She gained the section and let the pony carry her through the first scattering of trees. Brush reached out and plucked at her clothing. Something slapped against her face, almost blinding her, and adding to her sense of panic. A cry rose in her throat, but it was strangled when the pony caught a hoof in a snag and went down, throwing the woman over its head.

Lory found herself hitting the ground with

a sickening thump and then rolling until the bole of a tree stopped her with an equally sickening thud. Her pony squealed as she clambered to her feet and forced a way on through the brush, pushing it aside so that it sprang back on her with wicked pressure. She halted like a cornered animal when she reached a point where the dense under-growth shut out the light of the moon and stars. She heard her pursuer breaking through the tangle to find her; his curses rang in her ears.

Every breath burned Lory's throat like a brand; her breast rose and fell painfully as she stared around for some avenue of escape. There was a dark opening ahead and she went towards it, ducking, thrusting tree branches aside, disregarding the punishing thorns and snags.

Fresh horror raced through her when she saw a horseman coming through the fringe of brush on her left. She tried to scream, but managed nothing but a whimper of terror.

This newcomer left his saddle before he reached her, and she saw a big revolver clutched in his hand. A gun-shot erupted from the brush behind her, and the man in front of her threw a single shot in that direction. The brush flapped noisily and she gained the impression that Jim Ferraza was bolting.

She tried to streak away from the tall shadow that was drawing in on her. She had a brief glimpse of his gun swinging up menacingly.

He yelled a warning. 'Stay where you are!'

Something in the voice touched a responsive chord and Lory dragged to a halt, gaping as the newcomer approached. Then relief shuddered through her in little uncontrollable ripples.

'Oh, Del,' she cried. 'Is – is it really you?'

Then she was in the shelter of his arms, holding on to him fiercely as if she would never let him go.

Eleven

Del Pearce allowed the woman to hold on to him. Her tears wet his cheek and his fingers closed on her shoulders. A host of questions stormed through his mind. How had Lory come to be in this end of the range? Why was someone chasing her? Who was the person who had managed to turn her into a frightened creature seeking for a safe haven.

The moonlight let him see a shadowy form through the trees yonder. There was a horse as well, and even as he watched, a man hauled himself into the saddle. Del struggled with the woman.

'He's getting away...'

He would have shaken her off, but she held on to him, pleading brokenly: 'No, Del, no! Please don't leave me here like this. There might be more of them.'

Pearce looked keenly into her face. He had an idea that Lory didn't want him to go after the horseman. Already his mount's hoof-beats were hammering away into the night. Cattle bleated and lowed. A couple of beasts drifted past in a shambling run.

'What are you doing out here?' Pearce demanded.

'I – I thought I heard some men about the house,' she lied, resting her head on his chest. 'I just had to get out of bed and find out what was happening.'

'Ahuh!' If Pearce doubted her, he gave no indication. 'And that jasper who was chasing you just then – was he one of Overacker's boys?'

'I – I think so. I'm sure he must be. I saw them pushing some cattle and followed them across the river. I wanted to find out where they were going, and then one of them spotted me and came after me.'

There was an interlude of silence while Pearce thought that over. He could have gone after the fleeing horseman and overtaken him, discovered who he was. He believed that Lory had purposely held him back. She didn't want him to know who had been following her. Why not?

He said gruffly: 'It's safe enough now. You can find your own way home. I'm cutting out after that gent.'

'But, Del you can't leave me here. Don't you see that I'm frightened, that I'm hopelessly lost?'

'You're saying you couldn't find your way back to headquarters?' He found that hard to swallow.

'I know I couldn't. I never ride the country in the dark. Anyhow, he'll have got away by now.'

He asked her bluntly: 'Lory, did you know who he was?'

'Know him? Of course I don't know him. I wish I did.'

'All right,' he said, and went after her pony that was now standing near the fringe of scrub. He held the animal while she mounted.

A thought seemed to occur to her. 'What were you doing, riding around in the dark?' she asked him.

'I was having a nap under yon tree.' He pointed through the shadows. 'I saddled up when I heard horses running. And I must tell you that I didn't notice any riders pushing cattle from your side of the river.'

'Now I understand! You don't believe me, do you?'

'I didn't say that.'

'Del, are you working for Leon Overacker?' she asked bluntly.

'I'm working for nobody at the minute,' he replied. 'I'm looking for the man who killed

165

Hugh Temple.'

'Then you think this Tucson Kid is somewhere in the basin?'

'He might be.'

They were moving off, down towards the river, when Pearce heard hoofbeats cutting in from their right. They were being made by more than one horse and the riders were certainly pushing them along.

'Better smart up your pony, Lory,' he advised. 'That sounds like Overacker men coming to have a look-see.'

The woman gasped in dismay and urged her mount across the grass, streaking out in front of Pearce. Pearce turned his head, hearing the insistent drum-beat getting closer. His sorrel might manage to out-distance the cowboys, but Lory's pony would be no match for them.

'See those boulders up on your left,' he directed. 'Get to them fast and we might give them the slip.'

'What'll happen if they catch us?' she groaned in dismay.

'Then I'll do the talking. Remember that.'

They raced for the section of tall boulders, but it soon became evident that they were not going to be able to make it. The Split Diamond men had separated, and some of them were running almost level with the fugitives and closing in rapidly and pressing Pearce and the woman into the centre of a tight circle. A harsh cry caused Pearce to draw hard on his reins.

'Hold on there or we'll shoot!'

In spite of Pearce's warning to the woman to stop she kept going while he brought his horse down and lifted his arms. A cowhand went after Lory, and Pearce gritted his teeth when he saw the fellow leap from his saddle and bear Lory to the ground. She screamed, and one of the others swore in wonderment.

'Hell, that's a woman!'

'Yeah, and this is Mr Pearce,' another surprised voice cut in, and Pearce recognized Grat Jurado.

They tightened their pincer movement on him, their faces pale blotches in the moonlight. Pearce swung to the Split Diamond foreman and forced a laugh. 'Howdy, Jurado.'

'Howdy yourself, mister,' the other snapped testily. 'Now what in blazes are you doing riding round here with a woman at this hour?'

'There was shooting going on, Grat,' someone else chipped in. 'That's what made us call you.'

'What was it all about, Pearce?' Jurado demanded. 'And who's the hussy you've got?'

'No hussy,' Pearce flashed back. 'Mrs Temple.'

'No!'

The riders gasped as the cowboy came up with Lory. He, too, looked shocked and was giving Lory plenty of space now. 'Damn it, Miz Temple, I tell you I didn't know you were a woman,' he protested.

'You mangy cur,' Lory choked wrathfully. 'Why didn't you make sure before you jumped on my back ... Del, did you see it?'

'I saw it,' Pearce agreed tightly. Lory was as cunning as a fox and might try spinning some kind of tale that would make things look pretty bad for him. Jurado and his men just looked at the pair of them, waiting for an explanation.

'Well, mister, what goes on?' the foreman prodded finally. 'You got us out of warm blankets.'

'I'm sorry, Grat, but I was just–'

'Del and I were taking a ride,' Lory interjected. 'You see, Mr Jurado, Del came back to work for me today, and we were following a man we saw driving cattle in this direction.'

That threw the Overacker men off balance for a moment. All eyes were on Lory and each man was making his own private assessment of the situation. Jurado spoke up.

'Now, you'd better get something straight, Mrs Temple–'

'Oh, I'm not accusing Split Diamond of rustling my cattle,' Lory interrupted swiftly. 'But we decided to follow the rider anyhow. Then he lay in ambush and fired some shots at us. Del did his best to catch him, but he got away.'

There was no comment for a long minute, then Jurado said to Pearce: 'It happened like that, friend?' he queried.

'Yeah – yeah, sure, Grat. That's just what happened, except that I was just helping Mrs Temple out. I'm not really working for her. Not after tonight, I mean.'

'You know something, Mr Pearce?' Jurado murmured. 'You're a mighty strange fella.'

'Maybe so. I'm sorry you boys were disturbed.'

Grat Jurado put his back to him and said: 'All right, fellas, let's see if we can catch that rustler.' As his men moved off he glanced at Lory. 'Good night, Mrs Temple.'

'So long, Mr Jurado.' When they had all ridden off, she said to Pearce: 'I guess I said the first thing that came into my mind. I'm sorry.'

'Forget it. Lory, you told me there was more than one man with the cattle. Now you just told Jurado there was one. How come?'

It was difficult to read her expression in the darkness. She appeared to hesitate; then she laughed shakily. 'I was confused. There must have been more than one herder with the cattle, of course.'

'I'll see you back to headquarters.'

'Thank you, Del.'

They set off and reached the river at length and splashed through, then turned out towards the rising slopes of the Long T range. When they arrived in the front yard Pearce remained in his saddle for a while and looked around him. The ranch lay-out was in darkness. A dog barked once and then fell silent. Pearce slipped from his saddle and helped Lory to the ground. She touched his arm.

'Del, you – you'll stay here for the rest of the night? It's too late now to go anywhere else.'

'I'm sorry, Lory. I'd better keep moving. I've things to do.'

'At this hour?' A trace of mockery tinged her tone.

'The Tucson Kid might like the night

hours,' he told her. 'Anyhow, I'm not staying.'

She moved in closer to him and, before he could gather his wits, her arms went about his neck. He was immediately conscious of that wild stirring in his bloodstream and was gripped by a crazy impulse to yield to the woman's overpowering allure.

'This big house is so empty, Del,' she whispered against his cheek. 'Please come in.'

'No, Lory, no.'

She covered his mouth with her lips and he crushed her body to him. Across her shoulder he saw a glimmer of light at the corner of the house, as if a man was standing there, smoking a cigarette. He drew away from the woman and crossed the yard, hand hovering above his revolver. When he reached the corner of the building he hauled up. There was no one there. He sniffed, catching the smell of tobacco. He went on to the back of the house, and when he saw the cabin where Jim Ferraza would have his quarters he halted, eyeing the building. Lory came in at his side.

'What is it, Del?'

'I'm not sure.'

He left her and crossed the intervening space to the cabin. It was in darkness, but he fancied he heard a rustling sound inside. Something glowed at his feet, the still-burning stub of a cigarette. He put his shoulder to the door, but the inner bar was in its socket.

'Ferraza, are you there? Do you hear me?'

No answer, and he turned to look into Lory's white face. There was fear in her eyes now. Her lips moved without forming words. Pearce gave the door a heave.

'You in there, Jim?'

He heard a man cough, then, surlily: 'What do you want?'

'Ferraza, have you been out riding?'

'Say, is that Pearce? What in hell business is it of yours if I have? I'm trying to get some sleep, mister.'

Pearce clenched his hands. He stood back to throw himself at the door, then changed his mind, looked at Lory, and shrugged. He headed for the stable and the woman followed him inside. She watched him find a lantern and get it burning. He replaced it on its hook and went over to the stalls. The bay stallion was steaming and he met Lory's questioning gaze.

'Just watch him, Lory. He's a lot more dangerous than you figure.'

He left the stable and went back to the

sorrel horse. Lory clutched desperately at his sleeve.

'Del, please stay here and work for me, help me...'

'Sorry, ma'am, I've still got a heap of things to take care of.'

He rode out of the yard and wheeled into the north, soon passing beyond the woman's sight and hearing.

Jim Ferraza stood in the darkness of the cabin. He held his revolver at the ready should Del Pearce attempt to force the door. He breathed a gusty sigh of relief when Pearce finally moved away from the cabin. He watched from the window as Pearce and Lory went back round the corner of the main building, and shortly afterwards he heard a horse pulling out.

Now he gritted his teeth, fretting, wondering if it had been Lory who had trailed him across Split Diamond graze. But of course it had been Lory. He had recognized that voice when Pearce appeared on his horse and she had run to him. How much did Lory know of his activities? How much did she suspect or guess?

Ten minutes went by and still no one returned to the cabin. This worried Ferraza.

It tended to bear out his fear that she suspected him. Now she would watch his every move, or have some of her trusted men watch him – Sam Moro, likely. Maybe she would confide in Pearce and enlist his help. He swore, dragging out the makings and rolling another cigarette. From now on he would have to go easy, have to watch how he went about the business of stealing cattle. And this would have to happen just when he had managed to round up a dozen head of prime steers tonight!

In the morning, Ferraza hung around the bunkhouse after breakfast, hoping that Lory would come over to see him. Sam Moro asked sarcastically if the foreman had retired from work, and he flung Sam short answer, giving vent to the anger and anxiety that plagued him.

'Mind your own damn business, Sam.'

'I reckon I can do that,' Moro retorted crisply. 'You don't look so perky this morning, pard,' Moro went on. 'Out late last night?'

Ferraza strode over to the stocky man and thrust his face close to Moro's. 'What in hell do you mean by that?'

'Hey, you're getting edgy,' Moro replied coolly, his pale eyes level and unafraid. 'But don't try to saw it off on me, fella.'

There was still no sign of Lory when Ferraza saddled his bay and prepared to ride after the men. He moved round to the front of the main building and waited, slapping his thigh with his quirt. No one showed, and he headed off at length, eyes smouldering, wondering what in blazes was going on.

After supper that night, Ferraza went to the house to report on the day's events. Lory greeted him pleasantly enough and listened while he gave her the customary run-down. Her manner provided no inkling as to what had happened last night. Before leaving her, Ferraza decided on a bold stroke.

'Where is this fellow Pearce now, Lory?'

'Pearce?' she echoed abstractedly. 'How should I know?'

'But he was here last night, wasn't he?'

'Yes, he did pay a call, but he didn't stay. Why do you ask?'

'Oh, nothing, I guess.' He forced a laugh. 'But he did wake me up, hammering on the door.'

'He wanted to speak to you,' she revealed calmly. 'He didn't say why.'

Ferraza became truculent. 'Are you going to let him hang around like that?'

'Why not? He's trying to find the man who killed Hugh. Now, if that's all for now, Jim...'

Ferraza stamped out of her office, making no effort to hide his annoyance at the way she was treating him. He went to the corral and cut out a fresh horse and, minutes later, he swung round the corner of the house and rode off into the fading sunset flares.

Lory watched him from the gallery, then hurried to the bunkhouse and called Sam Moro out. She caught the cowhand's arm.

'Listen, Sam, this is strictly between you and me. I've reason to believe Jim is stealing cattle. I followed him last night and saw him driving off some Split Diamond stuff.'

Moro nodded grimly. 'That figures, Lory. He's been stealing our stuff, too, I bet. What do you want me to do?'

'He's just ridden off,' the woman explained. 'Go after him, Sam. See where he goes, what he does. Then come and tell me at once.'

'Sure thing, Boss.'

A short time later, Moro set off into the gathering shadows, riding hard, eager to get the deadwood on the man he was certain was nothing better than a heartless renegade.

Ferraza kept going steadily into the west for

a couple of miles, then he hauled in and looked over his back-trail. A wolfish grin plucked at his mouth when he heard the muted drumming of hooves coming in pursuit.

'Just like I thought, Lory,' he mused. 'You suspect me all right, and you're coming after me again to find out where I'm going. But this time you'll get a lesson you won't ever forget!'

Ferraza went on until he reached a point where the faint trail wound through a jumble of boulders. Here were grass and moss, always wet and slippery because of a spring that bubbled out from under a rock ledge. He rode the horse into a cleft where it would be completely hidden from the view of anyone coming through the rocks, and settled down to wait.

Tonight he would have it out with Lory Temple, and afterwards he would ride on into the hills to join the Tucson Kid's outfit. The Kid had hinted that he needed helpers and of being willing to recruit any likely rider who wasn't afraid of risking his neck in return for rich pickings.

The hoofbeats were coming closer, and Ferraza tensed, wanting to make sure there was only one horse coming up through the rocks. When he was sure of that he smiled bleakly, seeing how Lory had decided to make the trip alone. Likely she did not want to take any of her crew into her confidence until she was sure of her ground.

The rider came on, slowing now, taking it easy where the grass and moss ran slick underfoot. Ferraza peered round the edge of a boulder and frowned when he saw the blocky figure on horseback. This was not Lory Temple at all, but Sam Moro.

'You want me, Sam?'

At the sharp call, Moro tried to drag his horse back into cover; at the same time his hand shifted to the gun at his hip. Ferraza's gun spouted smoke and flame, and the echoes of the report rippled through the rocks. Moro tried desperately to hold on, still intent on getting his revolver clear, but his fingers were nerveless, useless.

Ferraza fired again, and the Long T rider fell over his saddle. The big horse spooked and raced on through the boulders, spilling Moro to the earth as it went.

Twelve

The death of Sam Moro and the desertion of Jim Ferraza were almost too much for Lory Temple to take. More cattle were being stolen from her grazing lands: hardly a night went past without a rider reporting the loss of stock.

Sheriff Tom Neel came out from San Felipe, and while he did everything possible to get a lead on the rustlers, he had no real sympathy for the woman. He had heard stories about her that did not go down well with a man who had a strict code of morals. Neel and his deputy had hunted for the man who shot Sam Moro, but were forced to the conclusion that Jim Ferraza had moved out of the country or joined up with the thieves.

Reports of rustling raids came from other parts of the range as well. Posses of cowhands were formed and spent days in the saddle, searching for the owlhooters. But always the rustlers were just one jump ahead.

One day a Long T rider came across a bunch of cattle on Split Diamond graze. An

Overacker man showed up, and reckless accusations were exchanged. Finally, the Long T man drew his gun and shot the Split Diamond cowhand in the leg. There were to be other incidents: Overacker's men trespassed on Lory Temple's territory in search of stolen beeves and discovered some of their stock running on the wrong side of the river. They rode up to the ranch-house, demanding to see Lory about it, and the Long T boss came out with a rifle and told them to clear off or she would start shooting. And so the tension between the two outfits increased.

In an effort to ease the situation, Leon Overacker and his niece rode over the Bighorn to visit Lory and have a heart-to-heart talk about the cattle stealing. But Lory took one look at the sweet-faced Willa and told Overacker she had nothing to discuss with him.

Willa had heard that Del Pearce was wandering around the basin in his search for the Tucson Kid, and she wondered if Pearce's lonely wanderings had anything to do with Lory Temple's ill-humour.

She and her uncle had arrived back at the river again when they encountered a couple of Long T men who regarded them coldly as they put their mounts into the water. Overacker spoke in friendly fashion and received a curt jerk of the head from one of the men, a rider he knew as Burt.

It almost seemed as if someone was deliberately engineering a range war between the two big outfits, and Overacker thought Lory Temple should be smart enough to recognize the danger. Still, he told himself, she could be perfectly aware of what was happening, but didn't care much who was hurt or who was killed.

On a distant hill-top, where he could view the front of the Long T headquarters clearly through the army telescope he carried, Jim Ferraza laughed throatily. He had just witnessed the visit of Leon Overacker and his niece to the Temple spread, and the fact that Overacker's call had been brief to the point of his not even dismounting from his horse showed Ferraza that his plan to make trouble between the two outfits was progressing steadily.

Beside Ferraza, the Tucson Kid squatted on his heels while he fashioned a cigarette. The Kid was growing a beard which gave him a wild, unkempt appearance. Ferraza had given up shaving, also, and he looked like the range hawk he was fast becoming.

The Kid took the telescope from Ferraza and held it to his eye. 'So the old gent didn't stay long after all,' he murmured.

'I told you what would happen if we played our cards right,' Ferraza enthused. 'They'll soon be blowing each other's head off and won't have time to look after their cows.'

'Maybe so,' the Tucson Kid grunted, dropping the telescope to the ground at his side. 'But that ain't your real reason for having them at each other's throat, Jim, is it?'

Ferraza grinned crookedly at him. 'You're a pretty slick gent, pard. But you've hit it on the head. I aim to see that Temple woman squirm. I want to see her brought to her knees.'

'Just because she wouldn't bed down with you, huh?' The Tucson Kid spat at a beady-eyed lizard and rose. 'Let's get out of here anyhow. We've work to do.'

'When are you meeting Carver?' Ferraza wanted to know. He lifted the telescope and stowed it carefully into its case. He moved to his horse.

'Saturday, in San Felipe.' The Tucson's Kid's lips bent in a grimace, the nearest approach he ever made to smiling. 'Another pouch of gold for you, friend Ferraza.'

'Yeah, and there's still plenty of beef hereabouts for the lifting.'

'Maybe.' The Kid sounded thoughtful. 'I'm getting a mite tired of this range, Jim. I aim to move out before things get too hot for comfort. Those cowpokes are spending plenty of time in the hills looking for us.'

'But what about Pearce? You going to keep ducking him?'

The Tucson Kid shook his head. 'I never forget a friend, pard. Nor an enemy. I'll get that one, never fear.'

'You figure he's still in these parts?'

'He's lying low if he is,' the Kid decided. 'But I think he's still hunting me on account of Hugh Temple.'

They moved off the hill-top and turned into the north, continuing to climb until they reached the timberline. They rose in leisurely fashion, like men with all the time in the world on their hands. Ferraza had learnt that the Tucson Kid had infinite patience. But once he sunk his teeth into something he never let go.

Full darkness held the wide reaches of the Bighorn Basin as Ferraza and another of the Tucson Kid's helpers, a man called Tobin, put their horses down the side of a gentle slope that led to the Split Diamond head-quarters. A can dangled on Ferraza's saddle-horn and he kept a hand to it, steadying it against the swing of his horse. His com-panion kept looking anxiously around him, on the alert for an Overacker nighthawk. The hour was late and Ferraza hoped the crew would have turned in.

The ranch-house and outbuildings loomed up at last, and Ferraza signalled his companion to halt where a clump of brush clung to a small knoll. He slipped to the ground, releasing the can.

'You stay here,' he ordered Tobin. 'If you see me coming on the run, cover me. Got it?'

'Sure thing,' Tobin grunted. He had no enthusiasm for this outing.

Ferraza left him and vanished in the gloom. The minutes passed and Tobin tried to imagine what the former Long T foreman was doing. He hoped he would make it quick in case some of Overacker's crew had been posted on guard. He was easing himself in his saddle when he glimpsed a pinpoint of light off on his right. The light grew as he watched. It shot upwards suddenly in a brilliant tongue of flame. Tobin heard the crackle of wood. He saw a shadowy figure coming towards him on the run and hauled his revolver out. The man was Ferraza, and he shouted as he drew closer.

'Get moving!'

Ferraza scrambled on to his own horse as a cry went up from the buildings. Someone yelled: 'Fire!' and someone else took up the cry. Ferraza waited for another few seconds, seeing how the fire was spreading hungrily. Overacker's boys would have their hands full dealing with it.

The pair raced back into the darkness and rode hard for half an hour. At the end of that time they were close to the spot where they had arranged to meet the Tucson Kid and his two helpers. They climbed a rocky bench and found the Kid and his men watching the distant glow.

'How does it look from here?' Ferraza chuckled.

'Pretty good. That fire will be seen all over the basin. It'll bring in every Overacker line rider to find out what's wrong.'

'Figure we should make the steal right now?'

'Why not?' the Kid rejoined. 'We'll grab what we can while the going's good. Then we'll get to drifting.'

'Right out of the basin?' Ferraza wanted to know.

'Sure. Len here says he came on a camp this morning. One horse. What does it sound like?'

'Del Pearce?'

'He's still on the range,' the Tucson Kid said in a reflective manner. He might even be trailing us around, waiting for his chance.'

'But why run away from him?' Ferraza queried. 'I thought you wanted to run into him.'

'I'll meet him all, right. But we'll deliver this herd to Carver's agent first. It's too big a thing to miss out on. I'm in no hurry getting to Pearce. You ought to know by now that I don't hurry things.'

Soon the five of them were making their way in loose single-file order across the bare, fissured benches. They circled the area where Lory Temple had erected her dam, and from there dropped to the lowlands, crossing the Bighorn at a shallow ford. So far they had seen nothing to alarm them, and the hour seemed indeed propitious.

The three-year-old steers were just where they were supposed to be. The Tucson Kid had kept his men scouting the range for the best beef and the most likely place to make a steal. He spoke a word and they split up, moving like wraiths among the sleeping cattle, speaking sharply, slapping ropes. The cattle rose, lowing and blatting. The men spread out now, working to the edges of the herd, closing in as the beasts heaved into motion and tried to get away from their tormentors.

Jim Ferraza used his rope freely, sending his big horse this way and that, cutting, chasing, pushing the beeves into a more or less solid mass. He spotted a rider coming in on his right, and at first thought it was the sour creature Tobin. But the man appeared agitated, anxious, and then Ferraza saw the gun whipping up to fire.

'Look out, men!' he yelled at the top of his voice.

The newcomer triggered as Ferraza clawed his Colt clear of leather. The bullet whined over Ferraza's cantle, making him jump and causing him to shoot wildly. The rider had been pulling back, seeking safety in discretion, but now his hands clutched at his chest, and Ferraza brought him from the saddle with his next burst.

At that moment the Tucson Kid galloped up. 'What in hell's happening...' He stopped speaking when he saw the body on the grass. Ferraza was out of leather and turning the man over with the toe of his boot. 'Know him?' the Kid queried.

'Don't reckon. One of Overacker's boys, I guess.'

The Tucson Kid went after the loose horse, soon overtaking it and grabbing the reins. He dragged the beast to Ferraza and told him to have a look.

The brand was plain enough on the flank without having to search for the neck brand. 'Split Diamond. That gun-fire'll carry some.'

'Get back to the steers,' the Kid ordered him. 'There might be more nighthawks about.'

They left the cowhand where he had fallen, turning his horse loose. It loped away through the grass, doubtless making for home.

Ferraza was grim-featured as he turned back towards the mass of cattle. The herd was bulked pretty solid now, pointed for the river and the high hills of the Bighorn country. They would need an hour at least to get well clear.

Ferraza was suddenly seized with a fit of trembling. It was the same kind of reaction that had followed the killing of Sam Moro. Did a killer ever get used to killing? One thing was certain he knew: there would be another accusing face waiting in the dark nights to haunt his dreams.

Thirteen

Del Pearce saw the glow of the fire from the spot he had chosen to make camp for the night, a place known locally as Pinnacle Peak. At the outset, the fire had appeared as a mere speck of light, and he had taken it to be a camp-fire away out on the flats. But then he judged distance and location and concluded it was somewhere in the locality of the Overacker headquarters, on the far side of the Bighorn, and that it was really a big affair.

He lost no time in gathering up his bed-roll and breaking camp. In short minutes he was in the saddle of the sorrel and making his way across the lofty plateaux that dominated this end of the range. He had searched every corner of the country for the Tucson Kid and his followers, but had found nothing but traces of the gang's passing.

It was all of an hour later when he rode on to Overacker grass and sent the blowing sorrel down towards the river. He missed the ford he had in mind and went through where the water was quite deep. On the other side he picked up his steady, space devouring stride once more.

He hauled in with a curse on spotting something lying in the grass and dismounted to have a look. The dark stain on the front of the man's shirt sent alarm streaking through him. This was Elmer Jorth, a Split Diamond hand. The body was cold, but Pearce was sure the man had been shot recently. He considered packing Jorth on the sorrel, but dismissed the idea. Some of Overacker's men could collect the dead cowboy.

Drawing closer to the ranch headquarters, he saw that the fire was dying, and had been coped with successfully before it had caused too much damage. Still, woodsmoke stung his nostrils, and burning timbers continued to hiss and splutter under the dousing of water. He soon saw that it was, in fact, the barn that had been burned.

A couple of weary-looking men were hauling buckets of water from the pump and flinging the contents on to the smouldering wood. Two men left to fight the dying blaze. Where was the rest of Overacker's crew?

He dismounted and slapped the sorrel on the rump, sending it away from the ring of heat. 'What started this?' he called to the pair.

One of them came over, an old-timer named Ben Keel. 'Say, you're that fella Pearce...'

'What happened? How did this start?'

'Some of the Long T crowd done it,' the smoke-grimed cowhand retorted. 'The boys headed off to settle the score.'

'But that's plain crazy,' Pearce cried. 'This isn't Lory Temple's work.'

'Boss sure thinks it is, mister. We've took enough from that bunch. Grat said he'd burn Long T to the ground before day busts again.'

'But he's wrong,' Pearce protested. 'Somebody else must have started the fire. Why, I found Elmer Jorth out on the range, shot in the head.'

'Elmer! His horse came in an hour ago. But how–'

Pearce left him and hurried round to the front of the house, coughing to clear the woodsmoke from his lungs. He wished to find out if Willa was here, and even as the thought registered he spied her on the gallery.

'Willa, is that you?'

It appeared as though she had been crying. She looked towards him for a moment, then shouted: 'Del, is it really you?'

193

'Well, I think so.' He failed in his attempt to sound cheerful.

He was not prepared for her racing down the gallery steps and throwing herself into his arms. Her eyes were frightened, cheeks tear-streaked. It was evident from the state of her clothing that she had been doing her share of fire-fighting. She clung to him fiercely.

'Oh, Del, please forgive me! It's just that I–'

'Don't spoil it,' he pleaded, holding her close. 'Your uncle has taken the boys to Long T, I understand. Do you believe that Lory Temple's men are the firebugs?'

'No, I don't,' she said quickly. 'We must do something to stop them.'

'Tell me exactly what happened,' he asked her.

'Someone sneaked up on the barn and set it alight. Mark Dugan saw a man on the hill-side. A man with a horse. He laughed, Mark said. He waited until the fire had taken hold before riding off. What – what are we going to do?'

'One thing's for sure,' Pearce answered grimly. 'You're staying right here, where you'll come to no harm.'

'No – please! Let me go with you. I – I

thought you had left the Bighorn country. Everybody believes that you have.'

'Well, I'll tell you something else for a fact,' he said huskily. 'I'll never leave these parts now. Not unless you leave with me.'

He released her and turned to call his horse. He refrained from looking at the girl again until he was mounted, then he reined over to her.

'Remember what I said. Stay right here until I get back.'

It wasn't until he had gone a mile in wild, headlong flight, with his heart threatening to beat through his ribs, that he realized he should have taken time to consider, that he shouldn't have let himself become intoxicated with Willa Overacker's nearness to the extent of not being able to think clearly. In his right senses, he would have taken the opportunity to switch horses, to leave a proper message for Leon Overacker should Overacker return to the ranch before he did.

Now, here he was, pushing the tired sorrel on another journey that would entail much hard riding and take them through more rough territory. He slackened the pace after a while, and finally let the sorrel choose its own stride. The beast surprised him with its powers of endurance, with its stoutness of heart. And when he reached the Bighorn again he let it have a short drink and time to blow before starting the long climb into the higher range where Lory Temple's Long T was situated.

All the way he was plagued by visions of Willa Overacker's tearful face. Her parting cry still rang in his ears and became part of the movement of the sorrel, and the rhythmic hammering of its hooves beneath him. Perhaps he should have told her about the cowhand Jorth, but he hadn't wished to add to her misery. The men fighting the fire would tell her about Jorth, in any case.

A distant rifle report jarred him out of reflection and made him concentrate on the possible danger up ahead. He was certain at this juncture that Lory Temple had taken no part in the arson attack. Whoever had shot Elmer Jorth had been disturbed after the fire started, and Pearce believed the real firebug was a member of the Tucson Kid's gang. Someone was set on throwing Lory Temple and Leon Overacker at each other's throat. Elmer Jorth had been a night-herder, and yet there were no cattle in the area where he had been killed. So it would appear that Jorth had been guarding stock that had subsequently been driven off by rustlers.

Another flat crack punctuated the stillness and he was followed by a steady fusillade of rifle fire. Pearce pushed the sorrel to the limit now, wanting to get to Leon Overacker and his men before blood was shed. He had no clear plan for stopping the fighting, but he would have to find some way of bringing both factions to their senses.

He came over a hill to see the dark outline of the Temple headquarters at the head of the high slope. By accident or design, Hugh Temple had chosen his ranch site well, as anyone planning an assault had to surmount that slope to get at the ranch-house itself. Even as he stared at the house a gun blasted out front. Pearce saw a lanky figure rise above a rock and shout something before dropping back into the shadows. Someone yelled angry defiance, and he knew that was Leon Overacker.

More rifle fire blazed from the Long T buildings, and Pearce realized that Lory's men would get the better of the fight according to the way things were shaping. He dropped from the saddle and left the sorrel, turning through the grass towards the jumble of rocks where the Split Diamond boss was taking cover. A man spotted him and threw a rifle up.

'Hold off, damn you,' Pearce yelled.

'Pearce...'

It was Overacker who recognized him, and without further ado Pearce made his way to the spot. Rifles and six-shooters roared, and bullets whistled dangerously close. Pearce flung himself to the ground beside Overacker. There was a depression in the earth here, and two other men were huddled down with their boss. The air was sharp with powder smoke. One of the men was Grat Jurado, and the foreman glared at him.

'Well, look what's blown in! Pearce, did Lory Temple send you over to spy out the land?'

'Don't be stupid,' Pearce snarled.

Jurado swung his rifle round to the house and let loose with two spaced shots. They heard glass smashing behind the answering shots, and the foreman showed his teeth in a savage grin.

'That's the medicine they made us take.'

Pearce gripped Overacker by the sleeve. 'You've got to call this off,' he cried. 'Quick, Leon, before somebody else is shot down.'

Overacker subjected him to a bleak look. 'I'm not sure what your game is, mister, but I'm playing this one my way. I've taken a bellyful from that damn woman. I even rode over and tried to talk peace with her. But she didn't want peace. She said she'd shoot any of my men who entered her graze after cattle. Then she tried to burn my place tonight...'

'That wasn't the Long T outfit,' Pearce reasoned. 'Hang it all, man, you must listen to me.'

He had the cowman's full attention at least. 'How do you know it wasn't Long T?' Overacker growled. 'Explain yourself before I get the notion you're nothing but a cursed trouble-maker yourself, Pearce.'

'All right then. But please listen: did you have cattle grazing above the north fork tonight?'

'Why sure I have. But what do you mean "had" cattle there? Elmer Jorth's night-hawking above the fork.'

'Jorth's dead,' Pearce enlightened him flatly. 'I found him lying in the grass. And there's no cattle there now.'

'What!' Overacker roared in disbelief. He would have stood up, but Pearce hauled him under cover as a steel-jacket spanged off the rock in front of him.

'It's the truth, Leon. Don't you under-stand what has happened? Some of these rustlers in the basin decided to set you and

Lory to fighting like cat and dog so they would have a clear run to grab your herd. It's one of the oldest tricks, and I'm surprised you fell for it.'

There was a fresh outbreak of frenzied shooting, during which neither side in the contest could claim a strike. Leon Overacker squatted on his haunches while his eyes drilled into those of the man beside him.

'Pearce, this isn't some smart trick of yours...'

'You've got to believe me. Damn it, would I hurt Willa?'

'Hell, you're on the square after all! I figured somebody was doing his damndest to make bad blood between the two outfits. And when Ferraza killed Moro and ran off–'

'Say that again,' Pearce gulped in amazement.

'Mean to say you didn't hear?'

'No, I didn't. I figured Ferraza for a rustler, sure enough. But I didn't know he'd killed Moro and left the Long T.'

'You ain't so slick after all then.' Overacker growled and spat. He thumbed under his hatband. 'There's a woman in there, mister. A woman, do you hear! And I'm making war on her. What sort of man am I? What sort of men are we all?'

'Easy.' Pearce counselled. 'The fire was the last straw for you and nobody can blame you for jumping to the wrong conclusion. But stop it now while you can, Leon. Call your men off at once. I'll try and get to Lory and explain.'

Overacker would have detained him as he wormed his way out of the depression, but Pearce just flung him a look and repeated: 'Call your men off.'

He ducked away into the shadows, making for the east end of the ranch-house. He had reached the veranda when a man rose out of the darkness, swearing in surprise as he whipped his rifle round. Pearce dashed across the few feet that separated them. The rifle exploded over his left shoulder as he crashed into the man, upsetting him and throwing him against the wall of the house.

'Hold it,' Pearce warned.

The guard swung the butt of the rifle at his head and Pearce ducked under it, at the same time driving a hard punch to the fellow's midriff. He swayed with a sharp expulsion of breath. Pearce hit him again, this time in the face, putting him to the boards. Then he raced on to the front door of the house.

The door was closed and he hammered with his knuckles. 'Lory, open up. It's me – Pearce.'

There was no response and Pearce watched anxiously while the Long T man gathered himself up from the end of the veranda. He hammered on the door again. Someone else appeared from the opposite end of the building, gun levelled. Then the door swung open and he made out Lory Temple's white face.

'Del...'

'Let me in,' he cried.

She stood aside to let him enter, then turned on him, eyes big with fear and wonder. 'Del, what are you doing here? What's wrong?'

'Tell your men to stop shooting,' he told her.

'But Overacker is attacking the ranch. Without any reason...'

'They've stopped shooting. I've talked to Overacker. He organized this war party because somebody tried to burn him out. It wasn't you?'

'Of course not! But I warned him that my men would shoot any Split Diamond rider who came on to my land. A fire, you say? His cattle were found on my side of the river. My cattle have been found on his side. It's all so hard to understand.'

'Not if you know what's going on,' Pearce declared grimly. 'There's a move afoot to keep you and Leon fighting while a certain gent gets away with your cattle.'

'Jim Ferraza?' she hazarded at once.

'Then you *were* trailing Ferraza that night when I found you?'

She nodded. 'I didn't want to admit it at the time. He killed Sam, when I told Sam to trail him and watch what he did. He didn't come back afterwards.'

'I've a hunch Ferraza's in tow with the Tucson Kid,' Pearce explained. 'They're behind this trouble-making. So get out there and order your men to stop shooting before Leon Overacker loses his patience.'

'All right, Del,' she said in a hoarse whisper, 'I trust you.'

He went into the night with her. The cowhand he had knocked down was waiting for him to show, and moved forward belligerently. Another one closed in from the opposite side, and Lory told them to back off.

'It's all right, Bob,' she explained. 'Overacker's men have stopped shooting. This has all been a terrible mistake. Tell the rest of the men to hold their fire.'

The pair slouched off, heads bent and guns at the ready. They had no intention of walking into a trap manoeuvred by the man they believed to be behind a lot of the trouble. Pearce stood by the woman until the spasmodic bursts of shooting tailed off. Eventually the gun-fire ceased altogether. Lory peered up into Pearce's face.

'Everything's quiet,' she said in wonder. 'It – it hardly seems possible. What happens now?'

'Simple,' he answered with a faint smile puckering his mouth. 'You and Leon Overacker can get together tomorrow, maybe. Smoke a peace pipe.'

'Maybe,' she conceded, laughing nervously. 'But if he comes here for a pow-wow, tell him to leave that niece of his at home.'

'I'll tell him.'

He brushed the back of her hand with his lips and dropped off the porch. He headed down the slope, watching the Split Diamond men rise from their various positions in the darkness. They followed him, not at all sure that their boss was doing the right thing by calling a truce.

Overacker strode forward to meet him. 'Did you ask her about the fire?'

'She knew nothing about it. You can take

my word for that, Leon.'

The rancher straightened his hat and stared up the slope. 'Does she want to dicker with me?'

'Later,' Pearce replied. 'Right now you'd better make tracks after the bunch that stole your beef.'

'What about it, Boss?' Grat Jurado queried. 'Finish this job or go after the wideloopers?'

'Job's finished, I guess,' Overacker said. 'What about Corby? He bad hurt?'

'Hole in his leg,' Jurado said. 'I plugged it and I figure he'll live.'

They brought their horses out and mounted. Pearce looked up the slope to see some shadowy figures moving around. Lory had ordered her men to see them off. The Long T men would remain on the alert, of course, just in case someone decided to leave his calling card. Pearce couldn't help smiling to himself. He considered he had done a pretty good job tonight.

Overacker's crew appeared anxious to get away at this juncture. One of them had the wounded cowhand called Corby riding double so that he would be brought home safely. Overacker joined Pearce again.

'Are you coming along with us?' he asked.

'I've a little chore to do on my own, Leon.'

'You'll call at the ranch later? There are still a few points we have to straighten out, you understand.'

'Sure, I understand.'

He watched them ride away and listened to their hoofbeats until the sounds faded out on the night. Then he fashioned a cigarette, got it burning, and headed for his sorrel. He knew that the Long T men were still up there, rifles and six-shooters at the ready. They were watching him, waiting, still suspicious of the stranger who had come among them, puzzled about his true motives.

At length Pearce rode away, reached the bottom of the slope, and chose a trail through the grassland. Find the Split Diamond herd, he told himself now, and you'll find the renegade Ferraza and the Tucson Kid.

Fourteen

He slept the remainder of the dark hours away in the high woods, and struck out at dawn to try and pick up the trail of the stolen Split Diamond herd. He started his search at the spot where he had found the body of Elmer Jorth, but cattle prints were everywhere at this point, and it was hard to determine the direction taken by the rustlers.

At mid-morning he ran into a couple of Overacker's cowhands and they chatted for a few minutes. One of the men said he had trailed the stock as far as the Bighorn. He was a dark-skinned man with more than a touch of Indian blood in him, and Pearce respected his comments.

'They crossed the river all right, then headed into the north maybe.'

'Maybe?'

'Your guess is as good as mine, Pearce. We're going to scout the country lying north of the San Felipe road.'

'They might drive to San Felipe?'

'Some of the southern ranches ship out from San Felipe, into Nevada and California.'

'It's worth a try,' Pearce agreed.

They left him and Pearce journeyed to the Bighorn, crossing the river and skirting the Long T boundary. The Split Diamond cowboy could be right, but somehow Pearce couldn't see the Tucson Kid trying to ship beef from San Felipe. He would be spotted there right away. Pearce had a notion that the rustlers would have a holding ground in the hills. They would blot the brands and sell to some agent with an eye to easy money.

With this theory taking root in his mind, he struck on into the northern tip of the Bighorn Basin. True, he had covered this section before, but there were numerous canyons up there that were pretty well grassed, and it would take months to make a thorough search of them all.

Two hours later he came on tracks in a mountain meadow.

He skirted the area carefully, then pushed off the meadow, still veering north. The character of the terrain changed, became rocky and unyielding, and the prints petered out altogether. At this point he allowed his instinct to take over and was rewarded when, on hitting soft ground again, he picked up sign of the rustlers having passed.

A long time later he came over the rim of a small grassy cup in the rocks. He arrived on the scene with a suddenness that took his breath away, and he hastily dragged the sorrel back off the skyline. That one brief, revealing glimpse had shown him cattle spread across the lush grass. He had stumbled on the rustlers' holding ground at last.

He left his horse in a clump of brush and approached the rim of the cup again carefully. He gained a sun-warmed niche and lay down to have another, better look. He had his second shock when he saw a small cabin almost directly below him.

Smoke trailed from the chimney pipe and he gazed around him until he spotted a couple of unsaddled horses grazing at the edge of the grass. Two horses. Which meant there might be only two men here, guarding the stock. He studied the small natural basin carefully in case there were other riders in the vicinity, but nothing else showed. He made a rough estimate of the size of the herd and judged there were about two hundred head. Quite a handsome haul for the Tucson Kid. But where was the Kid? And where was

Jim Ferraza. Were the two in that cabin at this very minute?

His pulse-beat quickened at the thought. If Ferraza and the Tucson Kid were the occupants of the cabin he would know soon enough. He wormed his way over the lip of the grassy cup or basin, glad of the fringe of aspens that would shield his approach to the structure. There were no windows at this side and he wondered at the rustlers being so careless. But it just showed how secure they thought themselves to be.

Pearce gained the aspens and hunkered down while he viewed the terrain. One of the horses, a big buckskin, had lifted its head and was watching him, tail switching this way and that. He eased his revolver into his right hand and considered the twenty-odd feet that separated him from the cabin. He drew a sharp breath and darted out, gun ready to blast at anything that showed. He reached the base of the building and sank down once more, listening. After a moment he heard voices.

The horse was shifting towards him, and he knew that it would soon whicker warning to the men in there. He moved to the corner, still seeing no window or door. The door must face down towards the grassed hollow. He crawled on until he was at the corner nearest the door. He saw a couple of saddles draped over a sturdy rail, with a coil of rope beside them. There was a pile of rubbish nearby, including empty cans, and he caught a whiff of the stench.

Something stirred at his back and he whirled to see the curious buckskin standing there. He motioned with his hand and the beast minced away, tossing its head and whinnying. Sweat rose to Pearce's brow. The men inside must surely hear the commotion. He could not afford to hold off any longer.

Pearce lunged at the door of the cabin and met a tall figure emerging. He had a vision of a bearded face and wide, surprised eyes. He brought the barrel of his gun swinging down on the fellow's forehead before he could duck out of the way. The man dropped without a word. Pearce heard a gusty curse in the cabin, and then he was leaping over the slumped form and pointing his revolver at the other one.

'Don't try anything!'

The second man backed off against a rough table. He was small, thin, and his features registered shock and fear. He had hauled his gun out, but he let it slip through his fingers to the floor.

'Don't shoot, mister,' he yelped.

'Who are you?' Pearce rapped.

'Lee Mercer.'

'Ah, I've heard of you, Mercer. Rustler! You working with the Kid?'

'He ain't here anyway.'

'Where is he, damn it?'

'I don't know. I–' Pearce grabbed his shirt and flung him hard against the wall. He slithered down on his haunches, raised his arms.

'Where is he? And I'd better tell you that I'm right out of patience.'

'In San Felipe,' Mercer panted. 'Him and Ferraza. They want to get rid of this herd quick. The Kid wants to pull out of the country.'

'That beef belongs to Split Diamond, doesn't it?'

'Some of it. Some is Temple stuff. You're Pearce, ain't you? What do you aim to do?'

Pearce got the feeling that he was trying to hold his attention. He heard a move behind him and swung to see the bearded man on his knees, a revolver in his hand. Pearce triggered as the rustler fired at him and then rocked back under the hot breath of powder smoke, hearing the bullet rip into the roof. Pearce was about to let loose with another shot when he saw the bearded man go down, a red blotch at his neck.

He glimpsed Lee Mercer scrabbling for his gun on the floor. He stepped on the man's hand, grinding the bones beneath his boot until he screamed. Then he backed away, motioning for the rustler to get up.

'It didn't work, pard, did it? You deserve–' He broke off, hearing hoofbeats hammering into the basin. His blood ran cold and Mercer gloated, small eyes bright with hatred and triumph.

'You're finished, Pearce! The Kid's come back sooner than we figured.'

Pearce was moving cautiously to the door when someone called: 'Hey, Pearce, are you there?'

Lee Mercer's face fell, and Pearce waited while Leon Overacker dismounted and entered the cabin. He was soon followed by two of his men. The rancher whistled in amazement.

'We followed you through the hills. I'd a strong hunch you'd lead us to something. Well, well, and who do we have here?'

'A couple of the Tucson Kid's gang,' Pearce told him. 'The Kid and Ferraza are in San Felipe. Take over here, Leon. You'll find some of your stock out there on the grass.

Long T beeves as well.'

'You heading for town?' Overacker wanted to know.

'I aim to go alone. You can arrange for the cattle to be driven back to home territory.'

'Good luck, boy,' the rancher called after him as he headed out to his horse.

It was approaching dusk when Pearce rode into San Felipe. He took the tired sorrel to the livery and ordered grain, asking the hostler to give the beast a good rub-down. Then he went into the yard and pumped water over his head and neck, and when he had dried off he returned to the main Street, looking for the cafe where he had eaten on his last visit.

Afterwards, he strolled around the darkening streets. If the Tucson Kid and Jim Ferraza were in town they would have to stay under cover in case someone put the law on the Kid. Someone was bound to remember the man who had shot Hugh Temple. But where should he start hunting for the pair?

He debated the wisdom of finding the sheriff, but dismissed the idea. Sheriff Tom Neel hadn't exactly impressed him when he had been here before.

He was coming out of a saloon called the

Silver Stirrup when he spotted a familiar figure standing against the wall. The man in the stovepipe hat gestured and Pearce joined him, glancing around to make sure they were not observed.

'Well, howdy, Cy. How goes it?'

'Hello, Mr Pearce. Thought you'd got itchy feet and left these parts. Say, the Tucson Kid's been here a couple of times since I saw you last.'

'That so?' Pearce's brows knotted. 'You didn't tell the sheriff?'

'Neel ain't such a close family friend. He talks a good deal as well, and I might have ended up with a bullet spoiling my style.'

'I've been busy,' Pearce explained. He stopped talking while two men came out of the saloon and went along the planking.

'I know where they are, Mr Pearce, strange as it seems,' Ford surprised him by revealing.

'Hell, you do! Right now!'

'Never pass up a chance to earn an honest buck,' the other chuckled. 'Right now, as you say. Cash on the barrel-head, though.'

'How much?'

'Cost of everything's going up, Mr Pearce. Why, I tried to buy a new coat the other day, and–'

'How much, damn it. I've no time to haggle.'

'Five bucks would see me all togged up like a real gent, I guess. I always wanted to look good and smell good. You know, like a...'

Cy Ford let the rest go unsaid as Pearce pushed five dollars into his hand. Then Ford pulled his hat down firmly, said conversationally: 'I knew sure as hell this morning it was going to be another hot day. In the Grand Hotel, just over the intersection. Heard they signed in as Bill Covey and Tom Wallace. Can you beat it?'

'Thanks, pard.'

Pearce touched the gun at his hip as he crossed a dark alley. He came up in front of the hotel lobby and peered inside. The lobby was big, brightly lighted. A large potted palm stood just inside the doorway. Pearce spotted a rangy clerk behind the desk. He strolled in, trying to appear leisurely.

The clerk looked up from the paper he was reading. 'Good evening,' he drawled, smiling at the newcomer. He had a kiss-curl greased down on his forehead.

'Look, Tex, I believe a couple of my friends are stopping here. Gents by name of Covey and Wallace.'

The clerk's brows arched. 'Everyone who came out of Texas wasn't necessarily a loose-mouthed gossip, you understand. Cattle dealers?'

'Right on the nail! They in now?'

'Hold on and I'll see. Say, you sure these people are your friends? I mean I've got a job to look after and everything...'

'Just wait till you see us all together!'

'Well, hell, why not? But I'd better go see if they're in right now.'

'Let me break the good news myself,' Pearce suggested with a grin. 'I'd sure like to give those two galoots a nice surprise.'

'That's all right with me.' The man consulted the register. 'You'll find them in number six. Top of the stairs and third door on the left.'

'Capital!' Pearce jerked his thumb and made for the stairway. 'How's the Lone Star state these days?'

'Ain't been home since Davy died at the Alamo,' the man returned dolefully. He jerked a thumb in acknowledgement.

Pearce mounted the steps swiftly. There was a narrow corridor at the top, with a single lamp burning in a wall bracket. The thick carpet deadened the sound of his boots and he soon drew level with the door

217

numbered six. He tapped with his knuckles and immediately heard a movement inside. A voice sang out. 'Who is it?'

Pearce tried the handle with his left hand. His right hand had fallen to the Colt at his hip. The door was locked. He rapped again.

'That you, Kid?' someone inside called.

Pearce recognized Jim Ferraza's voice and his mouth hardened. 'It's me. Open it.'

He listened to a bolt being drawn. The door swung back and Ferraza's bearded face appeared in the opening. His eyes bulged when he saw Pearce. He tried to slam the door, but Pearce had his boot in the gap and thrust it violently inwards, the force hurling Ferraza across the floor.

Pearce said briskly. 'Don't try anything foolish, Jim. You're coming to the pokey with me.'

'The hell I am!'

Pearce was raising his gun when Ferraza came at him with something bright in his hand. The naked steel caught the glow of the lamplight and Pearce swung aside as the knife flashed past his shoulder.

Ferraza turned about like a puma, fast and agile, driven by a tremendous fear. He brought the knife sweeping up in a cutting arc and Pearce managed to grip his wrist, his fingers digging in. They struggled desperately, Ferraza trying to force the knife down to Pearce and Pearce forcing it away from him.

They rocked over the room, locked in deadly combat. Ferraza gave a sudden, hard shove and Pearce felt the backs of his legs being forced against the edge of a sofa. He tried to maintain balance, failed, and fell backwards. Ferraza howled in triumph.

Pearce spun as the knife slashed at him. He caught Ferraza by the hair and yanked him on to the sofa. He pulled the man towards him, then spun aside again, this time tumbling to the floor. He heard Ferraza catch his breath in an agonized gasp, and rose to stand above him. The renegade was doubled over on the sofa, face grey and frightened, and then Pearce saw how he was trying to haul the knife out of his stomach. Even as he watched, Ferraza's eyes glazed and he shuddered convulsively before sliding to the floor. He groaned once and sagged down in an inert heap.

Pearce eared back the hammer of his gun when he heard footsteps pounding up the stairs. The clerk was shouting excitedly, and then a man was framed in the doorway, a lean, dark-faced man whom Pearce recognized immediately as the Tucson Kid.

'Pearce!'

The word was uttered in a high-pitched scream, and the Tucson Kid was grabbing for his revolver when Pearce's Colt roared, the noise deafening in the confined space. The Kid levered up on his heels, spun like a dancer, a harsh curse swelling in his throat. He fired from the hip and his bullet tore into the wall, sending lathe and plaster alike flying. Pearce triggered again. He felt vengeful, venomous. This was a score he had no compunction about settling. Still the Kid hung on to his grim purpose of defeating his enemy. He managed to drive another bullet into the floor before his body went slack and he keeled over into the corridor, his head cradled on his forearms as though he had merely fallen asleep instead of died.

Pearce stayed in San Felipe overnight and started for the Bighorn Basin next morning while the sky in the east was still grey and the air chill but infinitely clear and fresh. Sheriff Tom Neel was glad to see the end of the outlaw, of course but, characteristically, he made it clear that Del Pearce must not expect anything in the nature of a reward.

'Not even a medal,' Neel said with a trace

of sarcasm. 'One sidewinder less; one stupid cowboy cashing his chips too early. What do you figure it adds up to?'

'You add it up, mister,' Pearce responded curtly.

Still, he reflected later, he couldn't altogether blame the star-packer. He had felt like that once himself. When a man held on to a badge – or an ideal – for too long, he became hard and cynical. It was a lawman's disease, he supposed.

He rode along the wagon road at a leisurely pace until he reached the fork where the trails diverged, one leading to Lory Temple's Long T, the other to Overacker's Split Diamond. He reined in and smoked a cigarette, thinking of big John Halley. At Triple X a man would never be troubled with women like Lory Temple and Willa Overacker. And wasn't Halley fond of saying that he hadn't seen a rustler in years? Halley would welcome him with open arms. And yet...

His gaze shifted to the slopes that rolled away to the Long T headquarters and he gave a little serious thought to Lory. She was at peace with Split Diamond for the present, but who could tell when she would make another try to buy Overacker out? Well, there was no point in borrowing trouble.

Hoofbeats on the other side of the fork caused him to look along the trail that led to Split Diamond. Two riders were coming towards him, one tall and arrow-straight in the saddle; the other slender, with a cloud of brown hair flying in the breeze.

He waited until they came closer, until he could see Leon Overacker's anxious face that soon brightened in a glad smile, until he could practically see the tears of joy that glistened in Willa's eyes. Then he pushed the sorrel forward to meet them.